AINSLEY
KEATON

The Beachfront Winery

vinci
BOOKS

By Ainsley Keaton

Sconset Beach

The Beachfront Inn

The Beachfront Surprises

The Beachfront Reunion

The Beachfront Secrets

The Beachfront Girls

The Beachfront Sunsets

The Malibu Girls

The Beachfront Christmas

The Beachfront Retreat

The Beachfront Crush

The Beachfront Winery

Vinci Books

vinci-books.com

Published by Vinci Books Ltd in 2025

1

This work is a work of fiction. Names, characters, places and incidents are the product of the author's imagination or are used fictitiously. Any resemblance to actual persons, living or dead, places and incidents is entirely coincidental.

A CIP catalogue record for this book is available from the British Library.
Paperback ISBN: 9781036703806

Chapter One

Sarah

Ava was back in town, and was happier than Sarah had ever seen her. Ever. She was positively glowing as she served the various customers who came in to sample wine and buy bottles from the Sava winery. She was beaming as she talked to some of the regulars, including Joe, a firefighter who came into the winery all the time with his buddies, and Jean, a middle-aged woman who loved to bring her lady friends for some wine-tasting and lectures about all the latest wines Sava was offering.

Sarah knew why Ava was so darned happy - she was finally in love with a man who was not only her equal, but her age. As lovely as Ava's last love interest, Deacon, was, it just wasn't in the cards because of the age difference. Before Deacon, it was Christopher, the jerk who stole all Ava's money before coming back around and trying again. Ava kicked him to the curb for good after he confessed to having another family while he was married to her. The nerve of some people, Sarah thought, shaking her head.

While Sarah was thrilled for her sister, she suddenly realized that she was the only one of her friend group who was unattached. Mia and Quinn were going strong, as were Hallie and Conrad. Fiona, who was Sarah's new friend, was very happy with Jack. And now Ava was blissfully in love with Elijah, her step-brother-turned-soul-mate. Even Jessica, who was Ava's niece and one-time protegée, was married to Andrew, the pop-star who Jessica knew as a child and loved as an adult.

Love was all around her and she wondered if Cupid would hit her next. Not that Sarah was necessarily anxious for that. She had a wonderful life raising Julia and running the winery with Ava. She lived with Quinn and her daughter, Emerson, so she was never lonely in the evenings. Quinn and Mia were both great fun to hang with, as they often did in the evening, watching old movies on TCM, grabbing sushi from the restaurant down the street, going to the beach and watching the waves. But Sarah was starting to feel like a third wheel with Quinn and Mia, and she now had nobody single to run around with. And that felt a bit… strange.

She never imagined, when she was in high school and was the golden girl, the homecoming queen, the trendsetter, the girl who everybody looked up to and had boys falling at her feet, that she would get to the age of 54 with nothing but a broken heart to show for her romantic endeavors. She hated Nolan, the man who beat her down for years and years and made her afraid to love again. She fell in love with Max, but he was dying, which, Sarah had to admit, was a part of why she allowed herself to love him. It was a love with an expiration date, which meant she didn't have to truly commit to him. As painful as that was to admit, Sarah was still so terrified of committing to somebody that she could only become attached to a dying man.

She knew why. Nolan seemed perfect when she met him. Handsome, wealthy, worldly and seemingly kind, he swept Sarah off her feet. Sarah didn't even think about the moves she made after meeting him - quitting her job to follow him around, leaving her entire architectural career in the dustbin. The architectural career that she worked so hard for, getting a master's from Stanford and a bachelor's at the University of Missouri, was forgotten like a Craig's List free couch left by the side of the road. She had to quit because Nolan required his paramour to be free to travel the world and Sarah had always nursed a serious case of wanderlust. She didn't think twice about walking away from her first love, architecture, to indulge in her second love, travel.

And when it all inevitably fell apart after Sarah took the rap for her "friend" Lauren's drugs and Nolan sealed her fate by writing a letter to the California Architects Board filled with lies about her selling drugs to children, Sarah was stuck in a life with a man she now despised but had grown reliant upon because her career was well and truly dead. She thought that would be her entire life, following around a man she hated but who took care of her, but Nolan died a terrible death after suffering from ALS for several years and Sarah was free.

She didn't grieve.

She felt relieved.

Thank God Nolan passed away, Sarah thought with only a small amount of guilt. If he didn't, Sarah would've still been his prisoner. But she wasn't. She was living her best life with friends she loved. But, at the same time, her fear of getting involved with another man who would treat her like a possession to control kept her from looking at anybody of the opposite sex with any degree of romantic interest.

That day, she was busy waiting and bussing tables and selling their wines. Sarah was a wine expert, as she traveled the world, sampling wine wherever she sent.. It was a warm day in the middle of March, and spring was definitely in the air. Sarah loved the autumn and winter, loved the shorter days, the crispness in the air and the changing leaves, even though not every tree lost its foliage in Los Angeles during the wintertime. It made her just a bit sad when the winter was over and spring was upon them, but, at the same time, she was looking forward to tending her garden and growing roses, tomatoes, cucumbers and other flowering plants.

Nevertheless, Sarah somehow dreaded the coming of spring because it meant an end to the seasons she always loved. But, on the bright side, business certainly picked up with the warmer weather. March wasn't the warmest month in Los Angeles, not even close, but it was starting to warm up just a bit and people started to get spring fever. She noticed the outdoor dining was picking up all over Venice Beach, and her winery was seeing the spillover. And it would soon be June, the time of weddings and love. Sarah knew her winery would really start to jam during that busy season.

Sarah went over to a table where a well-dressed man was sitting. He was elegantly dressed in a silk beige shirt and light brown dress pants, no tie, with the top buttons undone, showing just a hint of chest hair. His dark tightly curled hair was cut close on the sides, long on top, and he was wearing a Rolex on his right wrist. He held a phone in his left hand and was talking rapidly in Mandarin Chinese, a language Sarah knew as well. The man was incredibly handsome, with green eyes, long eyelashes, a straight nose and bow-shaped lips.

Sarah got a whiff of the man's cologne, the heady scent she recognized as Aventus Creed, a top-drawer cologne featuring bergamot, black currant, patchouli, rose and and oak, amongst other tempting olfactory delights. She shook her head, feeling a draw to this handsome man unlike anything she'd felt for a long time, maybe ever.

Then he smiled at her, his clear green eyes shining, his straight teeth framed by full lips, and Sarah felt that smile like a beam of light. She involuntarily put her hand to her heart and felt it thumping beneath her fingers. She blinked and opened her mouth to ask for his order, but nothing came out.

"Hey," he said, his voice like thick, deep honey. "I'd like a bottle of your best Cabernet Sauvignon." He pointed to the menu at the bottle that Sarah and Ava sold for $500. "I'm waiting on some friends, so I need three glasses." Then he smiled again, and Sarah lost her breath.

Damn, that was a weird reaction for her. When she met Nolan, it was a different reaction than what she just experienced with this mystery man. She fell for Nolan because he was a gentleman at first, giving her a ride home when she needed it after being caught in the rain. She got to know him gradually, liking his mind and his manners. As for Max, she hated him at first because he accused her of being some kind of flaming liberal just because she didn't want to ban the same books he did, or, to be exact, didn't want to ban books at all. That she fell in love with Max came to an absolute surprise to her, not to mention surprising her friends.

But she'd never before experienced the kind of heart-pounding, lights-shining-from-above type of lightning bolt she just felt as she looked at this mystery man. Fiona, who was the resident matchmaker of Venice Beach, would no-doubt tell Sarah that she just met her soul-mate and that was why she had that reaction to the man. Sarah didn't necessarily believe in soul mates, the notion that souls travel throughout time and find one another again and again. But maybe she was wrong about that.

Sarah just nodded and wanted to ask if the friends he was expecting were male or female, but felt too nervous to ask that question. And she didn't want to be obvious about it. "I'll be right back out with that wine," she managed to croak out. "Can I interest you in any appetizers?"

He nodded. "Yes, a charcuterie plate would be nice," he said. "The one with the olives, brie, sun-dried tomatoes and fruit." He nodded. "That sounds like it would go well with the cab."

"It does," Sarah said with a smile. "That's my favorite charcuterie plate, actually."

At that, she walked back to the wine-tasting room where Ava was busy pouring more wine and chatting up several of the regulars who were getting drunk off Pinot Grigio and eating chicken wings. Ava smiled as Sarah came in. "Hey, sis, what can I get you?"

"The top-shelf cab," Sarah said.

"Oooo," Ava said. "I thought we'd never sell that bottle. Who's the high-roller?"

"A guy," Sarah said. "He's sitting outside, waiting on a friend."

Ava cocked her head. "Hmmm," she said as she studied Sarah's face. "You like this guy, don't you?"

Was she that transparent? Yes, she probably was. After all, Ava was her sister. Her sister was going to know when something was up.

She put her hands to her cheeks. "Yes," she admitted. "I

don't know, something happened when I saw this guy. I know nothing about him, other than the facts that he is incredibly handsome, dresses impeccably and smells delicious. And he has a voice like thick honey. If the man isn't a DJ at a smooth jazz station, he's missed his calling. But, other than that, I know nothing about him, but feel like I know him very well. Weird."

Ava nodded. "Sounds like Cupid finally found you," she said.

"Oh, come on," Sarah said. "I just said I don't know this man. That means I have no idea if he's any good. But he speaks fluent Mandarin Chinese, so it's safe to say he has some level of education because he's clearly not Chinese."

Ava grinned as she handed Sarah the bottle of Cab and the wine bottle opener. "Say what you want, but I think you've been hit by lightning. Finally. All my life, I've been wanting to see you hit by lightning and you never were. Lots of guys saw you and felt hit by lightning, but never the other way around."

Sarah knew that was true. She was always the heartbreaker, at least until Nolan, where she found herself the heartbroken. And she didn't like it. She didn't like it one bit. That said, Ava was right. There were many men along the way who told her she was The One. Men who Sarah thought in her mind were good for a short period, nothing more.

And Ava was also correct in saying that Sarah had never really fell for anybody before. Then again, she'd never met anybody who lit a spark for her the way this mystery man did just now.

She took the bottle of Cab and the charcuterie plate out to the man, who was now joined by two other people. They were all laughing and talking and the sound of this man's laughter lit Sarah up from within.

Sarah smiled, opened the bottle of wine, gave the cork to the man and poured a small amount into a glass for him to sip and give the okay for the bottle of wine. The man smelled the cork, took a sip, and smiled. "That's the stuff. That's what I'm talking about." Then he raised his hand for Sarah to shake. "My name is Silas Pierce. And who is serving this magnificent bottle of wine?"

"Sarah Flynn," Sarah said. "And, as you might have guessed, the bottle of wine you're enjoying is not one of our vintage. We've only been bottling wine for about a year, and this particular bottle is a 1984 vintage. That year was one of the best in the area in recent memory."

Silas nodded. "Yes, 1984 was a great year in this area for wine. The wines for that year were unusually robust, fruity, complex and rich. This bottle of wine is the perfect example of that."

At that, Sarah poured a glass for Silas' two companions, who both took a sip and nodded. "Delicious," the woman to his left said, swirling the burgundy liquid around in her glass. "Probably the smoothest glass I've ever had."

The guy to his right agreed. Sarah smiled and said she would be back to check on them. The group heartily said they would be looking forward to that.

Sarah went back into the tasting room and put her tray on the bar. "There's a woman with him," Sarah said dejectedly.

"And?" Ava asked.

"And nothing. I just wanted to state a fact." Sarah sighed. "Let's face it, the only men who will be available at this age will be carrying a lot of baggage or already would be in a happy relationship. Seems I missed my window for when that wouldn't be the case."

Ava laughed. "And what window was that?"

"You know, back in the day when everything was fresh and new and everybody didn't have 18 million exes and hadn't had their heart broken a bazillion times."

"And when was that?" Ava asked, clearly amused.

"I don't know. When we were 10, I guess."

"Exactly,"Ava said. "Let's face it, if you are a normal person, your heart gets broken a million times by the time you're 13. Maybe even younger. Not to mention, when you're young like that, you have a lot of other emotional issues that have nothing to do with the opposite sex and what they did to you. Maybe you don't remember it, but being young isn't always fun. You have so many pressures, you're not comfortable in your skin, so many insecurities, and high school is kind of a chaotic time. Personally, I think the best time is now. We are comfortable in our skin, we have money of our own, we have developed talents, and we're less likely to put up with bullshit."

Sarah knew exactly what Ava was talking about. While she was definitely one of the most popular girls in school, if not the most popular, it didn't mean she didn't have a ton of pressure on her. She did. She was constantly worried that people were going to talk about her behind her back, constantly worried she would fail somehow, and her failure would be so much more magnified than if she wasn't so well-known and well-liked in school. Worse than that, she never thought much of herself and never quite knew exactly what was expected of her. Everybody saw her as the golden girl, the head cheerleader, the school leader, the homecoming queen. All Sarah saw when she looked in the mirror was a girl who didn't measure up, who wasn't good enough, who wasn't worthy of all the attention. She had the worst case of imposter syndrome ever, but nobody ever knew this about her. She somehow managed to fake her way through school, acting the part of the girl who everybody thought she was, while secretly thinking she was a nobody.

Of course, she never told Ava this. Ava, at that time, would've rightly told her to quit whining. She had everything the awkward Ava ever wanted, so what problems did she have? Plenty, as it turned out, and she was never happy.

But now she was happy. Insanely so. Ava was right - it took time and maturity, but, like that beautiful bottle of wine she served up to Silas and his friends, the time and maturity made her finally feel beautiful and worthy, even though, in her mind, she clearly wasn't as physically beautiful as she was when she was 16. But her feeling beautiful was just a mind-set, and she would've had that same mind-set if she weren't objectively beautiful but quirky and strange, like she really wished she always had been.

Her feeling beautiful came from feeling happy and content, not by looking at a flawless face in the mirror. And that feeling was so much better than having everybody tell her how gorgeous she was when she felt anything but.

"You know, Ava, you're right. I'm really in a better place in my life to have a healthy relationship than I was when I was young and dumb and thought I knew everything. Thanks for making me see that."

Ava nodded. "Sis, you know that's what I'm here for. I'm always here to show you reality. And, in this case, reality is better than what you're thinking in your head. You have a lot to offer anybody, Sarah. You know this now more than you ever have before. So go forth in confidence that you will enrich anybody's life."

Sarah sighed. "Thanks for the shot in the arm. Now, to

subtly find out if Silas just happens to be single and ready to mingle."

"Mystery man's name is Silas?" Ava asked. "What a cool name. You don't hear that name very often, but it's really an amazing one. What does it mean, do you know?"

Sarah looked it up quickly. "Of the forest," Sarah said. "It's Greek." Sarah breathed heavily. "Of the forest." She closed her eyes, thinking of all the times she visited forests and the peaceful times she felt during these trips. The smells of leaves, pine and wet grass and the sounds of owls, crickets, frogs, streams and the wind rustling through the trees were peaceful to Sarah. How fitting that this man with the placid green eyes and golden skin had a name that echoed the forest.

"Silas Pierce," Sarah said, "is his first and last name."

Ava raised an eyebrow. "He's got a great name, I'll give him that."

"A great name for a sexy and handsome man," Sarah said dreamily. "Anyhow, I need to get to work. As do you." Sarah motioned to a group of 20-somethings who were coming through the door.

As Sarah was leaving the wine-tasting room, she bumped into Silas, who was coming in. She smiled and looked down at the floor. "You looking for the restroom?" she asked.

"No, actually. I was looking for you."

Sarah nodded. "I was just coming out to check on you guys. Is there something I could get for you?"

He walked over the bar and leaned on it and put one of his fingers up to his temple as he casually smiled at Sarah. "Yeah," he said slowly. "There is, as a matter of fact. I'd like your business card. I need a good sommelier who knows her stuff because I do a lot of entertaining and it's always a good thing to have the digits of a beautiful woman who knows her way around a bottle of wine."

Sarah nodded and went over to the bar, behind which she kept her cards. Then she casually wrote her cell number on the back. "My cell," she said. "You know, just in case you need an emergency bottle of wine for a fund-raiser or casual dinner with friends."

Silas smiled, his teeth brilliant and white. "You know, Sarah Flynn, I just might call this cell." He raised an eyebrow. "You know, maybe there's a casual dinner with a certain beautiful sommelier in the works. You never know."

Sarah felt herself blush. "Are you making an offer?"

"I am," he said, his voice sounding like buttery caramel. "You interested?"

Sarah nodded. "What did you have in mind?"

"What about dinner tomorrow night. Short notice, I know, but I have to fly out to China on the weekend and I'll be there for 10 days. But I don't like the grass to grow under my feet, so I thought I'd take a chance."

Sarah thought back to Silas' conversation in fluent Mandarin Chinese when she first came upon him. "China, huh?" Sarah had been to China multiple times herself, not just to the usual touristy haunts like Beijing and Shanghai, but also the small villages and rural areas where most tourists never dare venture.

"Yes," he said. "I'm an independent curator for art galleries around the city, and I'm working with LACMA right now on a contract basis. It's expanding their Asian art collection. I have some meetings with some museums in Beijing, as we're doing an exchange with them and they're offering several priceless paintings and sculptures on loan." "LACMA" referred to the Los Angeles County Museum of

Art, which housed one of the largest Asian art collections in the area.

Sarah put her hand to her heart. This man seemed too good to be true, at least on the surface. He undoubtedly had a PhD in art history or a similar area, so he had the intelligence, culture and education that Sarah craved in any man. He was also undoubtedly worldly, if he was a curator for the largest art museum in the area. That meant he and Sarah had travel and worldliness in common, and he was probably as curious as she was about the different peoples in the world.

Sarah took a deep breath. She didn't want to seem eager to have dinner with him, because a part of her still enjoyed the feeling of being chased. Yet, she knew she had to act fast, or this guy would be gone for 10 days and might not be back in to see her if she delayed him. And, unfortunately, the next evening was her turn to work late. But Ava probably would be more than willing to pick up Sarah's shift if Sarah asked her really nicely.

"Dinner sounds great," she said softly.

He smiled broadly. "Phew," he said, mock wiping his brow. "I saw you bringing my wine and thought 'no way would a beautiful woman like that be available,' but I took a chance and I'm glad I did."

Sarah smiled, thinking about how she thought the same thing about him. "Yes, I'm definitely available," she said. "My schedule is wide open."

"Okay," he said. "Pick you up tomorrow at 6ish? Or do you like to eat later or earlier?"

"6 actually sounds perfect," Sarah said. Back in the day, she used to eat a 8 or even later, but, these days, she found late dinners did nothing but keep her awake, so she was grateful for the opportunity to have dinner early.

Oh, the things that had changed for her now that she was in her mid-50s.

She shyly gave him her address and he grinned broadly.

"Well, I need to settle my bill." Then he gave her his credit card, Sarah ran it, and he left a $200 tip. "I have to go," he said. "But I'll be seeing you tomorrow night."

"Tomorrow night," Sarah said dreamily.

Silas left and Sarah turned to Ava.

"Wow," was all she said.

Chapter Two

Silas

Silas drove away from the winery because he needed to see his wife. Not that she was expecting him, but, at the same time, he always hoped that maybe she would be. Because, if she ever expected him, that would presuppose she knew who he was. And, for the last ten years, she hadn't known him.

Rita and Silas had a wonderful marriage. No children, but plenty of love. But early-onset Alzheimer's that progressed so rapidly that Rita went from completely normal to not knowing anybody in her life within one year, stole all of this from him. While Rita had periods of lucidity over the last ten years, they were brief and, lately, non-existent.

And Silas had been completely faithful to Rita all these years. But that all changed about a week ago when he saw HER. The woman he now knew was named Sarah Flynn and owned a beautiful winery in the Santa Monica Mountains. He saw her out and about at a café talking to two women who clearly were a couple. He felt stunned when he saw her, knocked off his feet in the best possible way. She didn't see him, but he saw her and overheard her talking about the Sava winery.

He left and immediately Googled the Sava winery, found out where it was, and made a date with his two closest friends to meet him there. He just wanted to meet the mystery woman he saw at The Bluestone Lane Venice Beach Café, not necessarily ask her on a date. But that's just what he did, and now, as he drove to the memory care facility that housed Rita - Ivy Park at Palos Verdes - he felt guilty for doing so.

This had been his life for the past ten years. Unable to move on because of his loyalty to Rita, yet confronting the reality that the woman he loved for so many years had no idea who he was. This wasn't like *The Notebook*, a book he loved to read Rita after she was first diagnosed and the two of them had to confront reality. That was a book, and this was life, and he felt conflicted, yet ready, to find a lasting love.

He got to the facility, checked in and went to Rita's unit. She was living in a luxury two-bedroom apartment that housed Rita and the private nurse, Amelia, who lived with her. He smiled at Amelia as he walked through the door of the apartment.

"Am," he said in an upbeat voice. "How's it going?" He gave her a quick hug.

"Silas," she said. "Rita is in the recreation room if you want to talk to her. They're showing a movie tonight."

"It's not *The Notebook*, is it?" Silas asked lightly.

Amelia chuckled. "No, I don't think so."

Silas found his way to the recreation room where about

20 residents were watching a romantic comedy that Silas didn't recognize. Rita was sitting there, watching the movie with everyone else, seemingly normal but Silas knew she wasn't the woman he married.

He sat next to her and put his hand on hers. She looked at him without recognition. She never remembered him, even though she saw him several times a week, because her short-term memory went back only several minutes. In other words, he would introduce himself to her, and she would acknowledge him, but then, not 30 minutes later, she would have no recollection of meeting him.

She smiled wanly and pointed to the screen. "I'm watching this," she said.

"I know," Silas said. "I just wanted to say hello."

"Hello," she said. Then she pointed to her name tag. "I think this is my name. Rita Pierce."

"My name is Silas Pierce," he said.

She smiled and then turned back to the screen.

Silas watched the rest of the rom-com that starred Sandra Bullock and Ryan Reynolds. He finally recognized it as *The Proposal*, a movie from the early 2000s, maybe from the 2010s, and, like all rom-coms, had a cute and happy ending. These movies usually made him sad, because his own happy ending was destroyed 10 years ago. And his wanting a different happy ending with a different woman was making him feel completely guilty.

The movie having ended, he walked Rita back to her apartment along with Miguel, one of staff members who escorted the residents to their respective rooms and apartments, and, after they got Rita to her apartment, he sat with her for about an hour before going home.

Then Silas felt the overwhelming sense of depression and despair he always felt after seeing Rita.

Only now, it was mixed with something he hadn't felt in a long, long time.

Hope.

Chapter Three

Sarah

Sarah got ready for her date, feeling more optimistic and excited than she had in a long time. She was so anxious to get to know this Silas Pierce that she was jumping out of her skin. Her friends were more than happy for her, and Quinn was in the bedroom with her as Sarah excitedly tried on one outfit after another.

"Sugar, you would look amazing in a potato sack, so anything you choose will look drop-dead gorgeous on you."

Sarah was nervously looking in her beautiful walk-in closet for just the perfect outfit. She felt like she was 15 again, looking for the perfect thing to wear because everybody always expected her to be decked to the nines wherever she went. Of course, she was more comfortable in blue jeans, a tank top and casual shoes or even Doc Martens when she was harvesting grapes, and a part of her wanted just to dress down for her date with Silas.

She finally took a deep breath. "You know, I don't know where we're going. He didn't say. So maybe I should just dress a bit casually yet dressy, just in case we go to a place by the beach and we end up walking along the shore later on."

She finally settled on a classic look - white sleeveless v-neck shirt, black flared pants and high-heeled Louboutin sandals. Her blonde hair was swept up, and her makeup was minimal. She kept her jewelry minimal as well - just a silver bracelet, a pair of dangly ruby earrings - ruby was her birthstone as Sarah was born in July - and a simple gold choker.

But, right before Silas was supposed to arrive, she got a call from him.

"Sarah, I'm so sorry," Silas said. "Something has come up and I can't make it. I'm truly sorry."

Sarah stiffened and felt tears come to her eyes. She was really, really, really disappointed. She was looking forward to that date like nothing she had for a long, long time.

She swallowed the lump in her throat. "I understand. Well, maybe when you get back from China, we can try again."

Silas was quiet on the other end of the phone, and Sarah's heart sunk. His silence was deafening. "Actually, Sarah, I think I might've done something rash and silly. No, that came out wrong. I asked you out because I couldn't not ask you out. Long story. But, to be honest with you, I'm not exactly free. I'm sorry. I'm so very sorry."

Sarah was devastated, and she couldn't quite figure out exactly why she was. She didn't know this guy. She saw him exactly one time. Yet, here she was, feeling she'd been dumped by the love of her life, a guy she'd been dating forever. *Come on Sarah, get a grip.*

"Okay," she said. "Well, I hope to see you around."

"Sarah wait-"

He said that, and Sarah hung up the phone.

Chapter Four

Silas

Sarah had just hung up, and Silas knew it was better just to leave well enough alone. He knew he was a jerk for calling off the date at the last second. But he had gotten news from Amelia that Rita was lucid. He really craved the moments when he could walk with Rita and talk to her just like they did when they were first married. When they could reminisce and bond. She had brief periods of lucidity before and cherished them.

Not only that, he knew his time with Rita was probably short. She had already been living with early onset Alzheimer's for 10 years. The lifespan for people in Rita's situation was only around 10 years. And Rita was already having problems with swallowing food. She was wasting away before his very eyes, so he had to take the chance to tell her everything he needed to while she had the capacity to understand.

A part of him knew Sarah was his future. Even though

he only met her once, and had seen her that night at the café without her knowledge, there was something about her that made him believe she was made for him. So, even though he was upset about breaking off the date with the beautiful Sarah, he knew in his heart they would work it out.

But, right now, he needed to put his present and his past to bed. He needed to be with his wife while he could, because there was a very big part of his gut that knew, absolutely knew, that this would be the last time he could talk to Rita and have her understand him.

He got to the facility, and walked through the door of Rita's apartment. She looked at him and smiled. "Silas, you're home. I made your favorite meal, coq au vin."

"With lots of garlic?"

"Of course. Well, I made it, but Amelia, I don't know if you know her, but she tells me she's my assistant, helped." Then she shook her head. "I don't know when I got an assistant, but she's really something special. I hope she stays."

"Yeah, I think she probably will."

"So how was work? Have you been working on a new painting?"

Before Silas was an art curator, he was an artist. He did okay for himself, especially after the Internet was invented and he was able to sell his paintings online. He dabbled, but his focus was on getting his Masters and PhD in art history, which he did at UCLA.

But, right after he got his bachelor's degree, also at UCLA, he lived on the beach and just painted for 2 years, living off his savings and hoping he could make it. He also worked part-time at a Thomas Kinkade gallery. But this was back in the early 90s, long before the Internet opened up an avenue for artists to sell their work, so he wasn't successful. When he realized he would never be the next Basquiat or even be a working artist, he enrolled in the UCLA advanced degree art history program.

To his surprise, though, his art eventually took off, so he was able to sell paintings for $20,000 and up, while working as an independent art curator. In addition to that, he found out about non-fungible tokens, which was a way that artists were making millions a year on their work. He did that as well, and was now one of the ones making seven figures a year on his art. So, he was able to parlay his love of art into curating for galleries and museums, while selling his own paintings for a pretty penny and making a fortune on them.

He was also a concert-level pianist, completely self-taught. He loved to play the piano when he was stressed and had some mad skills on the keys. So, he created a YouTube channel and uploaded videos of him playing the piano in various malls and airports, and currently had over 3 million subscribers to this channel. That channel was extremely lucrative, to the say the very least.

All of this added up to a seven-figure yearly income. He sometimes made as much as $5 million some years, other years, closer to $1 million, but always did extremely well.

But it wasn't always like this. No, there was a period where he and Rita were dirt-poor, but happy because they had each other.

"What painting are you talking about?" Silas asked.

"You know. That painting of the Statue of Liberty as a goddess," she said. "It's magnificent."

It was then that he knew what period Rita was living in. That was usually the disorienting thing whenever Rita was lucid - what time of their lives was she experiencing? Sometimes she would talk to him about his PhD program, which was what he was working on when the two of them got married after having dated for about ten years. Other times, she would ask him about his curator job, specifically asking him about his trip to Denmark. The Denmark trip happened right around the time she was diagnosed.

But, apparently, Rita thought the two of them were in their early 20s, their salad days of living hand-to-mouth in a Volkswagen bus they parked on the beach, back when you could park overnight and not be hassled by the beach cops. He had been accepted on an art scholarship, right about then, to UCLA's PhD program, but they were dirt poor. That was when he was working on that particular painting. If she thought they were living on the beach, she probably thought this tiny apartment was the height of luxury.

He smiled as he thought about his luxurious Malibu beach house, 10,000 square feet of glass and steel, right on the sand and water. How far he had come from those days living in a van! He thought about how Rita would think of that house, the house she had never lived in, because she had been in this memory care facility for so long. He felt sad again as he thought about how much Rita had missed.

"Work was great, baby," he said, calling her "baby" because that was what he always called her. "Now, what about that coq au vin?"

Rita used to be a very good cook and had considered doing it professionally before her diagnosis. But he knew Amelia probably did most of the work for this, because the residents couldn't be trusted around the stove or oven. Rita's period of lucidity could end at any time, so there was always the risk that the residents might slip back into their dementia while the stove was burning, which would be bad, to say the least.

Rita smiled coquettishly. "What about it, hot stuff?"

He got out several plates, silverware and glasses, and Amelia brought the food out. The smell of the chicken, bathed in a sauce of red wine and garlic spices, brought back so many memories for him. Memories of the two of them, right when Silas was starting to make it big in the art world, and Rita cooking this very dish to celebrate this first giant acquisition of a collection of Finnish art. Back then, the two of them lived in San Francisco, in a two-bedroom apartment that was part of a large Victorian home in the Pacific Heights.

"Rita," he said as the two of them dug into the tender chicken. "I wanted to tell you how I feel about you."

She nodded. "I'm dying, aren't I?"

Silas wanted to lie to her but knew he couldn't. He looked over at Amelia, who looked like she wanted to talk to him. He went over to her. "Rita, I'll be right back. I need to talk to Amelia. Your assistant."

He and Amelia went into the other room to talk privately. "What do I tell her?"

Amelia took a deep breath. "Her doctor thinks that this period of lucidity is known as terminal lucidity. It's different from the other times she was lucid. She's very clear about everything. She remembers her childhood, her early marriage to you, her sister and her parents. We've been talking about her past. She's been reminiscing all day with me. Her doctor explained to me that many dying patients become lucid like this right before they die. But it could be hours, days, or weeks."

"Do I tell her the truth, that she is dying? She asked me that question, point blank. What do I tell her?"

Amelia looked down at her shoes. "I think you should tell her the truth. She deserves to hear it."

Silas sighed. He knew Amelia was right. After all, if

both of them knew the score, they could definitely bond better. They could have conversations deeper, more meaningful, conversations that Silas had always taken for granted and never would again.

Silas went out to where Rita was sitting, and put his hand on hers. "Yes, Rita, you don't have much time left. So let's make these last hours special."

He sighed as he realized he had to be in China and was leaving the very next day. But he didn't know how much time he had left with Rita and wondered if he should cancel the trip. Well, not cancel, just postpone. There was a window of time – the collection for the museum could be delayed, and his boss, Becca, was very understanding. Becca's own mother died of Alzheimer's-related complications, so Silas knew Becca would understand if he had to delay the trip for a week or more. He had to get every last moment squeezed.

If he didn't, he knew he would be regretting that move for the rest of his life.

Chapter Five

Sarah

Sarah just stared at the phone in her hand with dismay. She was not used to being blown off. Not in the least. And it hurt. Bad.

She went down the stairs, Quinn following closely behind her. "Sugar, what's going on?"

Sarah shook her head. "I don't know. I was actually putting myself out there for the first time in a long time. Actually looking forward to date with a man. No, that's an understatement. I was looking forward to this date like I've never looked forward to anything in my life. And he just called and blew me off."

She suddenly realized she probably shouldn't bother. Why should she? Her life was perfectly fine without a man. Yes, everybody in her friend group was now attached to somebody. Everybody but her, but she was just going to have to be the third wheel or the fifth wheel for the time being. And that was okay with her. She especially enjoyed hanging out with Quinn and Mia. Quinn and Mia went out of their way to make sure Sarah didn't feel like a third wheel. And, when they went out together, they simply look like three women out on the town. Having a girls' night.

Of course, when she hung out with Ava and Elijah, Ava's new beau, it was a different story. Hanging out with them did make her feel like a third wheel, so she didn't like that as much. It was hard to see the two of them mooning over each other, so Ava tried to make as much time as possible for Sarah, just the two of them.

As for Hallie, who often hung out with Conrad, it was much like with Ava and Elijah, although Sarah got along with Conrad much more than she did with Elijah. She liked Conrad's dry wit, his intelligence, and his artistic ability. Conrad was a very interesting person to Sarah. Elijah had his qualities, that was for sure, but he was much more serious than Conrad, much less irreverent.

Sarah admitted she was looking forward to double dating with her sister and Hallie, but now she thought that probably wouldn't happen. And that disappointed her.

"Well, sugar, when do you think you'll see him?"

Sarah shrugged. "He's going to China tomorrow for 10 days, so, who knows? Maybe he'll get in touch with me when he's back in the states, or maybe he won't. Probably won't."

Two days later, when Sarah went to the bookstore owned by Fiona Kennedy, who was a new part of the friend group and had her own love connection with a guy by the name of Jack, she got a most unpleasant surprise.

Who was in the bookstore, purchasing the latest Tess

Gerritsen, but Silas Pierce himself. Sarah saw him but he didn't see her. He was too busy talking to Fiona, who was working behind the counter. They were talking about the poetry slam that would be occurring that evening. Apparently, Silas was a bit of an amateur poet along with every thing else he seemed to have going on in his life.

And then she heard something that stunned her.

"My wife, Rita, will be with me tonight. I don't think you've met her."

"No, I haven't. But I'm really glad you're going to be coming around tonight for the poetry slam. They're really a lot of fun." Fiona was packaging up the book, while her beau, Jack, wheeled over to the espresso machine and made Silas a cup.

He had a wife? Sarah felt her heart thumping. Damn! She knew it. She knew he was too good to be true. So that relationship she was creating in her head was just that – in her head. She should've known better. Here she was, in her mid-50s and still getting screwed over by a member of the opposite sex. Not that that was necessarily something Sarah had experienced on a regular basis, like her friends, but she had her share of heartbreak.

She ducked behind a bookshelf and took a book off the shelf and pretended to read. If Silas managed to see her, she didn't want him to think she was spying. But that was exactly what she was doing - spying. Lurking around. Skulking, if you will. She wasn't exactly cloak and dagger, but, at the same time, she didn't want to be obvious either.

"I'm definitely looking forward to it. My wife loves to do this kind of thing. It's something we've always shared."

"Well then, join the fun. Maybe you can be a judge. Or maybe you just want to be a participant. Either way, it's a blast."

Silas nodded and then looked out the door. "It's a beautiful day," he said. "It's a great day to go to the beach. Anyhow, I'll be seeing you tonight."

Silas left, and Sarah went over to Fiona. "Do you know that guy?" She asked her.

"Silas? Yeah, I've seen him in here a few times."

"Does he often do the poetry slam thing?"

"No. Not that I know of. But he was talking about his wife, and I guess she likes it. Why do you ask?"

Sarah shrugged. "No reason."

Fiona furrowed her brow. "No, I think there's another reason why you're asking me these questions. Out with it."

Sarah sighed. "It's just I thought I was going to have a date with him, but, come to find out, I guess I won't be. And he gave me some story about going to China today. Actually, he was supposed to go to China yesterday. But yet, here he is, going to a poetry slam tonight with his wife." Sarah put a fist to her forehead and shook her head ruefully. "Why are men such shits?"

Fiona smiled. "I don't know the answer to that question. I know there's a lot of dogs out there. But there are some good ones, too." She looked over at Jack dreamily. "Like Jack."

Sarah knew Jack a little, and she had to agree with Fiona – Jack was one of the good ones. Maybe he was one of the last good ones, along with Elijah and Conrad, of course. Jack was very sweet and was totally over the moon about Fiona. And why shouldn't he be? Fiona was a superstar actress in her former life, as popular in the movies as Taylor Swift was with her music, but she left it all behind to live a normal quiet life running a bookstore and tending to her sweet Jack. She had every reason to be stuck up but was far from that.

"Jack certainly is a good guy," Sarah agreed. "Anyhow…"

Just then, Silas came back into the bookstore. He saw Sarah and immediately looked down at his shoes. "Sarah," he said sheepishly.

"How was China?" Sarah asked, an eyebrow raised.

"That trip was uh, postponed."

Sarah looked at Fiona who was staring at Sarah and Silas with wonder in her eyes. Sarah shook her head. She knew that look Fiona was giving them. It was her patented *you-two-are-soul-mates-did-you-know-that?* look.

No, Fiona, you don't know what you're talking about. Sarah crossed her arms in front of her. She was unbelievably angry and had no idea why. Again, she didn't know this man from Adam. Yet, as she looked at his handsome face, she felt a rage threatening to boil over like a pot of water on the stove.

"Postponed," Sarah said. "Maybe your wife made you stay home."

Silas' eyes got wide and his cheeks reddened. "Sarah, you don't understand."

"Oh, I think I do. I think I do." But did she? None of it really made sense, once she thought about it. It wasn't like the jerk took her out, wined her, dined her, and bedded her before dropping the inevitable bomb on her head. He simply made a date with her, a date he broke at the very last second.

"No, you don't," he said.

"Then explain it to me," Sarah said, tapping her foot.

He just shook his head. "I have to go," he said. "I just came back in to find out what time the poetry slam was, as I forgot to ask Fiona about it."

"7 tonight," she said. "Hope to see you there."

"See you there," he mumbled and then went out the door.

Sarah turned to Fiona. "What an ass," she said. "An absolute ass."

Fiona looked at Sarah. "Sarah, that ass, as you call him, is your absolute soul mate."

Chapter Six

Sarah

Sarah shook her head. "I knew you were going to say that. I knew it. When you looked at the two of us with that moony look you get, I knew you were going to tell me I belong with that man."

"Yes," Fiona said. "And that's just what I am telling you. You belong with him. And he belongs with you."

"Oh? Maybe somebody should tell his wife this information. You know, the wife who will be here tonight at the poetry slam with Silas?"

Fiona looked desperately at Jack, as if Jack had the answer. "Jack, do you know anything about Silas, the man who was just in here?"

Jack shrugged. "No, I've just seen him in here a couple of times, looking for books. Why?"

Fiona looked back at Sarah. "I don't know what to tell you," she said. "But you know how I see a light shining between two people who need to be together? Well, I saw that light between you and Silas and it was the brightest I've seen yet. The two of you have traveled through time and space, again and again. I know this. I have these special abilities and you have to know that you and Silas are meant to be."

Sarah cocked her head. "Great. Just great. I traveled through lives with a guy who is already married to somebody else. That's just lovely."

Sarah suddenly felt like crying. It wasn't like her life was a mess or even lacking. It wasn't. But a part of her knew what Fiona was saying - Sarah did feel an instant pull to the man. Like she had never felt before.

Fiona just sighed. "I don't know what to tell you, Sarah. I really don't. All I know is that you've met your soul mate. It's Silas."

Sarah raised an eyebrow. "Oh, maybe he's open to a throuple." Then she smiled. "Guess it doesn't hurt to ask." She was joking, of course. Alternative lifestyles weren't for her.

She put a book on the counter and Fiona rang it up. "Oh, the new Grisham. It's a good one. Hope you like it."

"I usually do," Sarah said.

At that, Sarah went out the door and got on the famed Venice Beach boardwalk. The usual people were rollerblading, biking, walking dogs and eating ice cream.

She saw Silas in the distance, standing by the water and staring at the waves. He wasn't moving. He had his hands dug into his pockets and just stood there. Like he was thinking really hard about something.

Sarah felt the temptation to go over to him. Maybe go up to him and bitch him out. Tell him just how much patience she had for games. She was in her mid-50s and was all out of f's to give. She had played the game before, had the game played on her from time to time, and thought it was high time games ended.

She went over to walk towards Silas, but then saw two women, one of whom came up to him and put her arm around his back. Sarah took a deep breath and then went back to her car.

Silas could pound sand as far as she was concerned.

Chapter Seven

Silas

Of all the people, in all the world, that Silas didn't want to see in that bookstore, that person was Sarah. Sarah now knew he was married. And that he wasn't in China.

He wanted to explain to Sarah what was going on. That he was married, but his wife was in the final stages of Alzheimer's, which was why she was so lucid and able to do things with him she hadn't done before.

He wanted to explain it, but couldn't bring himself to. It was so personal what he was going through and he didn't know Sarah.

Or did he? A part of him knew Sarah very well. As in, he felt he knew her better than he'd known anybody in his life. He felt this connection to her that was so strong it was palpable. Like it was something he could reach out and touch.

He left the bookstore, feeling confused. Why was Sarah put into his path at this moment? Was there something to him meeting her right now? It wasn't fair. He had to give Rita his time because he knew her time was running very short.

He had arranged for Rita to get out of the memory care place for the day. She was going to join him at the beach, along with Alicia. And then they were all going to the poetry slam that evening.

Rita and Silas went to poetry slams all the time when they were younger. That was one of Rita's favorite things to do. They had never even been to one, had never even heard of them, at the time they accidentally walked into one at a café back in the early 2000s. They had such a blast that evening, listening to poems and improvisations and seeing the people judge and cheer for them. That inspired Silas and Rita to work on their own poems, and, for weeks on end, they presented these poems to various slams around LA.

Now, here was a poetry slam, which was the perfect way for him and Rita to spend an evening. He wanted to do everything he could for Rita while there was time.

Just then, Rita and Amelia came up to him. Rita put her arm around his back and put her head on his shoulder. Silas and Rita knew that there was probably only days before Rita went back into her twilight world, and, from then, it would only be a matter of time before he lost her completely.

"Silas," she said. "Aren't you looking forward to the slam tonight?"

"Yes," he said with a forced smile. "Of course I am. It's something we always looked forward to, so it will be fun, as usual."

She nodded. "You know, Silas, you're young. Really young."

He grinned. "55, babe, that's not so young."

"You know what I mean. Your parents are in their 90s, both of them. They're both healthy as horses. You don't have any major disease in your genetic tree. You probably will live another 40 years. You need to live those years out happy. With somebody who will love you for all the wonderful qualities you have."

He put his arm around her. "Rita, babe, don't talk like that. These next few weeks-"

"Days," she said. "Probably. I've doing research on what's going on with me - terminal lucidity. I know the score, Silas. Don't get me wrong, I'm grateful for this time. Like you don't know how much I feel grateful for these last few moments with you. But, Silas, we need to talk while there's still time."

He nodded. Oh, he didn't want to level with her. Didn't want to tell her he already had her replacement in mind. Her replacement. In mind right now, as he had his arm around her. How fair was that? He was already looking beyond the horizon, already thinking Rita would be nothing but a memory in a few days, weeks if they were lucky. His mind wasn't on the present, it was on the future. That wasn't fair to the woman at his side.

"Rita, I don't want to talk about this."

"I think you do," she said. "I think you need to, Silas. And I need to hear it. I need to hear you will be okay after I'm gone. I need to die happy, Silas, and the only way I can is if I know you'll be taken care of."

Silas took a deep breath. No, he wasn't going to confess to Rita that he made a date with a woman he felt an instant connection with. That if love at first sight existed, it happened for him and this mystery woman Sarah. That he loved her, but, in his soul, he always thought there was somebody out there who he got to his very core.

"Baby, don't worry about that," he said.

Rita shook her head angrily. "Dammit, I *am* worried about that. Don't you see? You think you're doing right by me by spending all this time with me because you know it's just a matter of time. And I love you for that. I do. But I need to know you have a future with somebody. Maybe you don't know just yet who you want to be with for the next 40 years, but I need you to tell me you know you will be with somebody."

Silas took a deep breath. "Okay," he said quietly. "There's a woman. Her name is Sarah. And I met her and felt something."

Now Rita was smiling big. She clapped her hands together delightedly. That was what she did when she was really happy about something - she clapped her hands together rapidly. "Now we're talking. Tell me about this Sarah."

He sighed. "You really want to hear this?"

"Yes! Yes! Yes, I want to hear this. Dammit, Silas, give me the deets."

"Well, she owns a winery in the Santa Monica Mountains. With her sister."

"And?"

"And, she's beautiful and smart and seems like a sweetheart."

"Okay," Rita said. "I need to meet her."

"Whoa, whoa, whoa. What do you mean, you need to meet her?"

"I mean I need to meet her. I need to make sure she's the one for you. Because I know you. You're a man. You might get sucked in by a pretty face. A pretty face that might end up stepping all over you. So, yes, I need to see her for myself. Meet her and see what I think."

"Oh, boy," Silas said. "Rita, I can't-"

"Stop. You can and you must. Now, get on your phone and call her. Now. Let's have dinner tomorrow night. Assuming I make it that far."

"Are you sure?"

"Positive."

He took a deep breath. "Okay, then. But, tonight, it's just you and me and the poetry slam."

Chapter Eight

Sarah

Sarah was working at the winery when Silas appeared, his wife in tow. At least, she assumed it was his wife. The woman was extremely slim, probably only weighed about 95 pounds, with dark curly hair, big blue eyes, and a strong Roman nose. She resembled Debra Winger in the movie *Terms of Endearment.* She looked right at Sarah and smiled.

"Sarah," Silas began. "Can I talk to you?"

Silas had called Sarah several times, but Sarah let all his phone calls go to voicemail. He texted her to say he was going to be at the winery with his wife, and Sarah did not respond to that text. So, here he was, with his wife, and Sarah had no idea what was going on. Maybe he really was looking for a throuple. Perhaps he was into polyamory. Sarah didn't really know, but what she did know was that she was not into that kind of thing. Not that there was anything wrong with that lifestyle. It just wasn't for her.

Sarah took a deep breath. Silas and his wife had arrived

at the winery at 9 o'clock in the morning, way before the place was about to get busy. So Sarah had a moment to speak with Silas.

Not that she wanted to. She really wanted to just turn her back on the whole situation. She couldn't imagine anything good coming from getting involved with this man. He lied to her about going to China and he had a wife. Why would she want to give him the time of day?

Still, she reluctantly decided to talk to him in private. There was something in her gut that told her she needed to hear him out. So hearing him out was what she would do. She was a reasonable person. She wasn't one to blow people off if they were going to make a good-faith attempt to communicate with her.

"Sure," she said. She had on a large straw hat, gardening gloves, boots, jeans and was ready to tie the grapes to steel wire. Harvesting was still months away, and the planting was already done. It was now time for the "awakening," where the plants were shooting up and needed reinforcement. She also needed to check the vineyards to ensure she didn't need to replace the wires, poles, tensioners and all the rest. In short, she needed to ensure the vines were strong and supported and any structural failure could be addressed.

Ava was behind the bar, getting ready for the rush. Sarah went and found Ava to tell her what was going on. When she walked in, Ava was talking to Silas' wife. The wife smiled at Sarah and Ava nodded to her. "Go and talk to Silas," Ava said to Sarah. "I think you need to hear what he has to say."

Sarah just nodded. She went back outside, where Silas was waiting for her, his hands stuck in his pockets. He smiled at Sarah shyly, and followed her out to the field of grapes. The sun was beating down because it was an unusually hot day for March - 80 degrees.

She went along the steel wire, tying up the grapes, Silas following along. He couldn't help her with her work, as he wasn't dressed for such a job - he was dressed in light linen pants, a button-down dress shirt and a pair of high-dollar Prada leather shoes. But Sarah wasn't going to accommodate him. She was still angry about being blown off and was going to show this in the most passive-aggressive way possible.

"Go ahead, tell me what you need to tell me," Sarah said brusquely as she went from one vine to the next, tying them to their posts and examining each one carefully.

Silas was quiet for a few moments. "I think you need to know some pertinent information about Rita, my wife," he began.

Sarah raised an eyebrow, the sweat stinging her eyes. She wiped it away and continued on with her work.

"Rita is in the final stages of early-onset Alzheimer's. She is lucid at the moment, because apparently's Alzheimer's patients, right before they die, sometimes become lucid. Nobody really knows why this happens, and nobody really knows how long it lasts. It could be hours, days, weeks at the very most. Probably, it will only be a matter of days, if I'm lucky. In other words, Rita is terminal. She probably only has a few days left to live."

Sarah swallowed. Now she felt tears coming to her eyes. She felt an enormous amount of guilt. Here she was, thinking of her own feelings, and her own anger. How selfish was she? Here this poor woman was coming to the end of her life after having suffered from the cruelty of not knowing the people around her and living in a twilight state of confusion, and Sarah was worried about a broken date.

"Was this why you didn't go to China after all?" Sarah asked. She was now standing up and facing him. She wanted to hug him but was now sweaty, so felt too self-conscious.

He nodded. "Yes." He took a deep breath. "I wasn't prepared for her to become lucid. She'd been lucid a few episodes in the past, usually for only a matter of hours. But the life span of an Alzheimer's patient is typically only a decade, and she's been suffering from this horrible disease for over 10 years. She's been having difficulty swallowing. Not now that she's lucid, she hasn't had those problems. But, as I said, it's only a matter of time before she slips into her final moments. I don't know when it will be."

"So she became lucid out of the blue and you postponed your China trip?"

"Yes. That's exactly what happened. The China trip was all ready to go, but then Rita became lucid, so my boss allowed me to postpone the trip until…"

Sarah knew the end to that sentence. It hung in the air, neither of them wanting to speak the truth that Silas was now just waiting for the inevitable to happen.

"So now she's here," Sarah began.

"Yes. She wants to meet you." He paused. "She wants to know I'm going to be okay after her passing. She wants me to have a full life for the next 30 or 40 years or however long I have left. And Sarah, I know this is going to sound weird, and if it does, I apologize. But I felt something when I saw you for the first time. Like a lightning bolt hit me. You brushed me when we met, our skin met when you shook my hand, and I felt electricity shoot up through me like I'd never felt before. It was like a static charge. I don't know how to explain it, but I have this feeling you and I might go the distance."

He looked down at the ground, obviously embarrassed to be talking like this to a woman he didn't know. But Sarah was right there with him - she felt the exact same way about him. Like it was love at first sight, if that was a thing. She wasn't sure if it was really a thing, but she believed it now.

And Fiona told her she and Silas were meant to be. Fiona did have a special ability to match up soul mates. That was her thing. So, with Fiona saying these things to Sarah, it only added to the feeling that Sarah was supposed to be with this man.

"Silas, don't feel embarrassed about saying these things," Sarah said. "Because I felt it too. Between me and you, I felt it."

He smiled his beautiful smile, and Sarah smelled the scent of his high-dollar cologne. She thought that, if something happened and she never saw this man again, if she ever smelled that particular cologne again, it would bring her a sense of sadness that things didn't work out the way she wanted them to. She might smell that scent forever and always associate it with this man.

"So, what are you trying to say about Rita?" Sarah asked.

"She wants to meet you. She wants us to have dinner together, the three of us. Tonight. I hope you don't have much going on, because it has to be tonight. If we put it off for another day, it might be too late. And I really want her to die happy. I want her to die knowing I'm taken care of."

Sarah nodded. Of course she would do that. If Silas' wife had a final request, and Sarah was able to honor it, she would. Again, she felt a sense of injustice that the poor woman not only was going to die at such a young age, but she apparently had knowledge of her impending demise. What did that feel like to know you only had a matter of hours, days, weeks at the most to live? It had to be a scary thought for anybody.

Sarah herself was afraid to die. She didn't know what was on the other side. Or if there was another side. Perhaps this world was all there was, which made the injustice of dying at such a young age all the more acute. So she tried to put herself into Rita's shoes and felt a sense of despair. Anything she could do to make Rita's life happier, she would do. She didn't know her from Eve, but that didn't matter. What mattered was that Rita was a human being.

"Okay, why don't we go ahead and have dinner together tomorrow night?" Sarah said. "That would be nice."

Silas smiled. "Rita really loves seafood, so the Dudley Market would be our choice. It has fresh Baja seafood and it's on the canal. I love the atmosphere there, and the food is amazing."

Sarah took a deep breath. "Well I probably should go in there and talk to Rita. I saw her talking to my sister. I would like to learn more about her."

And Sarah wanted to learn all she could about Rita. It would tell her a lot. One of the things it would tell her is what kind of woman Silas was looking for. Yes, both of them felt the instant pull to one another. They both met and felt hit by lightning, as it were. But Sarah knew that maintaining a long-term relationship took more than just having an instant attraction to one another. It also meant having similar values, similar beliefs, and similar temperaments. So, if this Rita person was completely opposite of her, and they had a happy marriage, that would tell Sarah that it was possible they wouldn't make it over the long term.

She knew she was being cautious, but at the same time, she also knew it was important to be that way. She wanted to always go into every relationship with her eyes wide open.

And this was no exception, even though she felt so attracted to this man.

She went into the tasting room, where Rita, another woman who Sarah didn't know, and Ava were all chatting and laughing. That was a positive sign, in Sarah's view. That meant Ava liked this woman, because Ava was not somebody who could fake enjoying somebody's company. She wasn't somebody who could glad-hand with the best of them, as it were. If Ava didn't like you right off the bat, Sarah could usually tell.

Sarah went up to the bar and sat next to Rita. Rita looked at Sarah.

"I guess Silas told you all about what's going on?" Rita said matter-of-factly. "I'll bet you're relieved. You probably thought you were going to be part of a throuple." Then she laughed, as if she was thrilled to death to know that particular slang word.

Sarah wondered how she did know that word. According to Silas, Rita had been living in the twilight world for the past 10 years, and that word had just recently come into vogue.

Sarah laughed as well. "Well, maybe you guys would've wanted that, but I wouldn't go along with it. Not my style." Then she put her hand on Rita's shoulder and squeezed. She tried to hold back tears as she looked into this woman's eyes. Rita was either the bravest woman Sarah had ever met or was in a bit of denial. Yes, Rita intellectually knew she only had a matter of days before she went into another twilight world, and, shortly thereafter, would cease to exist. Yet, there she was, standing and smiling as if she had no cares in the world at all.

"I was telling Ava about the wonderful time Silas and I had last night at the poetry slam. You really should do that with Silas in the future, Sarah. He's very much a poet. He won in the urban category. He's very good at the language of the street. He grew up in south-central, you know. Single mother, but his mother was a saint. Silas always got the best grades, was always a bookworm and artist. You really need to see his art, too."

Silas was standing next to Sarah and smiling. "Rita always did think I hung the moon. But I'm not special. My mom, she's special. I've had an easy life, at least compared to hers."

Rita playfully punched Silas on the shoulder. "He's so modest all the time. I guess because he's so brilliant at so many things, in his world, everybody's brilliant at poetry and art and music and academics. He went to UCLA on an art scholarship, but he could have just as easily gone on a music scholarship. He's brilliant on the piano. Composes music, just like John Williams. For that matter, he could've gone on a football scholarship. He definitely had his pick."

Silas was standing next to Rita, shaking his head. "Now, now. You're exaggerating just a little bit with football thing. I was a pretty decent tight end at South Central High, but, trust me, I wasn't good enough to go on a scholarship anywhere."

Rita laughed. "Maybe that's true, but you were offered a musical scholarship to Julliard. Yes, the man I married is an absolute genius in so many ways, but what I love most about him is that he rubbed my feet after a hard day waiting tables, he makes the most wonderful chicken piccata I've ever tasted in my life, and he's kind." Then she laughed. "I could never kill a bug in the house because Silas believed they had a right to life. He would carefully put them on a sheet of paper and make sure they landed on grass outside. We had bird feeders all over the house, because he loved feeding birds and consider them friends. He would go to the lake and name the ducks he could recognize. One time, an opossum showed up at our back door, wanting his help, and he found that opossum and brought her back to health and made sure she got back home safely. And all the lizards in the backyard were really his friends."

Rita was certainly selling her man. And Sarah could see the love between Rita and Silas. She felt so sad for the poor woman. She swallowed a lump in her throat as Rita went on.

"So, Sarah, I know what an absolute gem my Silas is. We were very happy for a long time, I guess until I got my diagnosis and according to Amelia, here, my assistant, I haven't been recognizing people for a long time. I could just imagine how sad this made Silas all these years. It's just been so unfair to him, but Amelia says he's been at my side just about every day he's not out of town for some kind of business trip. He's been faithful and loyal to me all this time that I haven't even been able to say his name because I never knew it."

Rita was smiling, but Sarah could see the sadness behind her eyes. "Rita, thank you for telling me these things about Silas. And I'll be looking forward to getting to know you tonight, too."

"Oh, yes. No offense, but I'm going to be grilling you. Not that I think that you are anything less than wonderful. You're obviously beautiful, and Ava told me how kind you are. How accomplished and intelligent you are. So, on paper, you're wonderful. I just want to make sure you're right for my Silas."

Sarah just nodded. What could she possibly say to this woman? She felt tongue-tied. There is a part of her that really thought she would be stepping on Rita's toes if she openly flirted with Silas or even assured Rita she felt she and Silas were meant to be. So, she just nodded.

"Go ahead and grill," she said. "I've got nothing to hide. Well, aside from the fact that I was in a long-term relationship with an emotionally abusive man, and I married another man without hardly knowing him because I wanted to be a mother to his daughter Julia after he passed away, I don't think I have too many blemishes."

Why did she say those things? Especially the part about Nolan. Now Rita was going to think that Sarah was a woman without judgment. She was book smart, but emotionally smart? Not so much. That was going to give Rita a big red flag. Yet, at the same time, she felt comfortable enough around this woman to admit her flaws.

Rita nodded. "Well, I think all of us have used poor judgment in our lives. I'm sure there's a story behind why you would stay with a man who emotionally abused you."

Sarah sighed. "Yeah, but it's not a good one."

Silas put his hand on Sarah's shoulder. "Okay, Sarah, I'll see you this evening at the Dudley Market. I think Rita needs to rest a little bit for going out tonight. Don't you, Rita?"

Rita nodded. "Sure, Silas, I do need to rest, so thank you. See, I told you Silas was a considerate gentleman."

The two of them left, and then Sarah shook her head. "Why did I say those things to her? She didn't need to know those things. Now, I'm going to have to explain about taking the fall for Lauren's drugs and how Nolan sabotaged me to the architectural board, and how I was a convicted felon for all those years because of the two of them. Things I didn't want to go into."

Ava put her hand on Sarah's shoulder. "Sis, don't worry about it. I was talking to Rita while you were outside with

Silas and she's a wonderful and very understanding woman. I have a feeling your honesty with your past will reassure her more than anything. As long as you make it clear that what happened in your past is in your past, and you're a completely different person than you were before, I don't think she'll have a problem with it."

"I hope you're right. I think the reason why I said those things was because, I don't know, they're just still so top of mind for me. Like I've been obsessing about all those wasted years with Nolan. I'm so filled with regret, it just comes out of my mouth at times it shouldn't."

Ava shook her head. "At some point, sis, you have to forgive yourself. Forgive yourself and stop thinking you're not lovable. Because you're lovable. You're a wonderful sister, wonderful friend, and an amazing mother to Julia. Everybody who knows you loves you. So, please, just stop beating yourself up. You deserve the moon. I know it, everybody knows it. It's time you know it too."

Sarah just took a deep breath. "Silas really loves that woman," she said. "And I'm pretty sure he probably listens to her when she says something. If she doesn't like me, that might be all she wrote for me and Silas."

Ava just laughed. "Cross that bridge when you come to it."

Chapter Nine

Silas

"So, what did you think of Sarah?" asked Silas on the way back to his home. Rita was in the front seat of his Range Rover and Amelia was in the back. He was going to take the two ladies to his Malibu house. He wanted Rita to see the house because he wanted her to know just how successful he had been over the years. He knew that would make her happy, because, even though the two of them were very happy when they lived on the beach in a van, Rita knew at that time that Silas wasn't entirely happy with his station in life.

"She's gorgeous, that's for sure. She looks like Charlize Theron."

"Yeah. But what else do you think about her?"

Rita shrugged. "I think the two of you have a lot in common. Ava told me Sarah's always been the golden girl, the one everybody looked up to, the leader in her school, the homecoming queen, the cheerleader. It's just like you in your high school. You were always the leader, too. You have much more in common with her than you ever did with me."

Rita was, in her high school, the loner who loved to paint. That was what drew him to her in the first place – she had one of those booths set up on the beach where she sold her paintings. He loved her art. She was only 16 at the time, he was 18, and he was impressed that she had the wherewithal and gumption at such a young age to set up a booth to try to sell her paintings. It wasn't until later that he found out that the reason why she was selling her paintings at the age of 16 was because her family desperately needed the money. Her mother was suffering from ovarian cancer and her father was dead. She had a little sister, aged 12, and, because her mother really couldn't work, there wasn't much food in the house. Rita was a very good artist, so she tried very hard to make enough of the living to pay for food and utilities. Her mother's disability check covered the rent, although barely.

When she told him her sad story, he fell in love with her. She was doing all she could to help her family. She wasn't in school, she was manning the booth by the beach, evading the truant officers because it was that important to her to sell her art.

It made him sad that Rita had such a terrible time when she was very young, what with her father dying she was only 12 and then her mother eventually passing away from the ovarian cancer when Rita was 21. And now, here she was, 54 years old, having suffered from early onset Alzheimer's for 10 years, and about to die. It just seemed that tragedy seemed to haunt the poor woman, followed her around like a dark cloud. Yet she simply was a good person. And all the tragedy that plagued her throughout her life didn't change that.

"Is that so bad? That Sarah was the golden girl?"

"I don't know. I just wonder what she knows about suffering and about people who don't have it so great. It does kinda concern me that she's the kind of girl that had everything handed to her because of the way she looks. Sometimes girls like that just expect things. Just expect people to cater to them. Not that she's like that, but, I don't know, I want to find out for myself. I'm just looking out for you, Silas. I just want you to find a woman who's going to know what she has in you, instead of expecting things that shouldn't really matter in life."

Silas knew what Rita was talking about when she said that some people just expected things that really shouldn't matter in life. By that comment she meant material things. A big house, a nice car, lots of money to go on vacation, that sort of thing. Rita was never into any of that. So, it seemed that she was clearly leery that maybe Sarah was the kind of girl who would want all those things. That maybe Sarah was the kind of person who would just expect him to provide for her. A gold-digger.

Silas knew what Rita was talking about – some very attractive women expected people to shower them with lots of gifts. He remembered one time, when he was a bartender, there were a group of girls drinking all night on some guys' dime. They were happy to hang out with the guys as long as the guys were paying for their drinks, but as soon as those guys had enough and refused to pay for their drinks anymore, they were gone.

Those women were just a small example of the larger problem of gold digging women who use their wiles and looks to lure people in and use them. But Silas knew in his heart that Sarah was not that kind of woman. He didn't exactly know how he knew this for a fact, but he knew it. So he just knew Rita would have to see for herself.

He put his hand on Rita's hand, and then he brought her hand to his mouth and kissed it. "Babe, I know you're looking out for me. You know I have stuff I never had before." And, at that, they approached his home. His home was a 10,000 foot glass and steel modernist home that was right on a beach. Rita looked at this home, and her eyes got wide.

"Oh my God, Silas. You really have made something of yourself." She smiled. "You know I never worried about that. I was really happy living with you in that rusty old van on the beach all those years ago. But I knew you really wanted to be rich and famous. It looks like you are."

He just nodded. "Yeah, my artwork is doing really well. I certainly couldn't pay for this house on a curator salary." And then he paused. "And, I have a YouTube channel that's going really well. I have over 3 million subscribers." He got the idea of posting videos of him playing the piano in various malls and airports after seeing other people do the same and become very successful in attracting subscribers. He had concert-level skills and put them to use. It still astounded him how many people were willing to subscribe to a channel where there's a dude just playing the piano. As long as said dude was extremely proficient on the piano, and it didn't hurt if the guy looked good as well. While Silas was a very modest man, he also knew the ladies loved him and the way he looked. He wasn't going to lie to himself - he would use his looks to his advantage.

Rita cocked her head. "You're doing well on YouTube, huh? Good for you. I've watched some YouTube with

Amelia. Seems like a fun channel. How do you make money on that?"

"Well, if you have a lot of subscribers, you can sell a lot of ads to run on your channel." There were other ways, too, like affiliate marketing and selling products from his on-line store, but he didn't want to go into all that.

Silas also made millions selling his art as non-fungible tokens. He figured out how to do that on-line. He was self-taught for most of the ways he sold his talents in art and music because he was always motivated to make something of himself. He knew there were plenty of other people out there who were more talented than him, but didn't know how to make money with what they were doing. Silas was ahead of the game because he figured out all the income streams he could.

Of course, he didn't tell Rita about the NFTs. She wouldn't understand what they were and it wasn't important.

They went into the enormous house, with super high ceilings and his artwork everywhere on the walls. The only reason why he had his own artwork on the walls was because he had very distinctive taste in art, and his own artwork fulfilled that singular taste of his. He loved certain other contemporary artists, he wasn't that much of it egoist, but no artist appealed to him on every level. Of course his own art appealed to him on every level, and he was living there alone, so of course he would decorate the place exactly how he wanted it.

Rita walked around the house, in complete awe. "Boy, Silas, you really have come a long way from that van on the beach." She looked at him. "I'm very proud of you. I guess I need to tell you that. Because, as we both know, it's just a matter of time before I can't tell you how proud I am of you."

Silas felt an overwhelming sense of sadness. Every time he thought that he soon would not have Rita in his life anymore at all, he wanted to cry. "I know, Rita. Let's not think about that right now."

Amelia, for her part, was also walking around the beautiful house and marveling at the paintings on the walls. "Rita always told me how good of an artist you were, but, wow! You really have a knack."

Amelia was referring to the few times in the past where Rita was lucid. Also, when Rita was first diagnosed and admitted into the memory care place, she had her long-term memory intact, while her short-term memory was completely gone. So, at that time, Rita remembered the days living on the beach and the art he painted during this period.

After Silas gave both Rita and Amelia the tour of the enormous home, the trio went out the back door and listened to the waves coming in. His view of the ocean was amazing. He knew it and felt grateful for it. He knew he was very fortunate to be living the life he was living, especially because he knew his wife wouldn't share in any of it. He thought again about how unfair it all was to her. Why was he given so much, and she was given so little? Why was the quirk of fate so cruel to some people and so good to others?

Rita smelled the salt in the air and smiled. "This place really brings me back. I mean, I know we didn't live in such a luxurious home back in the day. We just lived in that van on the beach, but the smell of the salt in the air and the sound of the waves, it really reminds me of those early days."

Silas smiled. "You know, we couldn't live on the beach

now. They kick people out now at like 2 o'clock in the morning. And that goes for just about every beach in the area."

Rita shook her head. "That's silly. I mean, I guess I know why they do it. They want to discourage homelessness and all that, but who really cares if someone wants to live on the beach? It's not like there's going to be all kinds of crime going on in between the hours of 2 AM and 6 AM, or whatever time the beach opens in the morning. And then they wonder why there are so many people who live on the streets downtown. Just let people live on the beach and they won't sleep on your doorstep."

"Preaching to the choir. But there are other changes I think are good. Like nobody can smoke on the beach anymore."

Rita scrunched up her nose. "Smokers did it to themselves, you know. If they would just not throw their butts on the beach, maybe they could still smoke on the beach. I know, I know, you don't want them throwing their cigarette butts in the trash. But did they ever think that maybe they could just take a coffee can full of water and put their cigarette butts in that? No, they never thought about that, so they just threw their butts on the beach for the seagulls to eat. You know seagulls get addicted to that stuff because of those slobs who didn't care enough to actually dispose of their cigarette butts responsibly."

"True that. True that."

At 7 o'clock, Rita and Silas were waiting for Sarah at the Dudley restaurant. Silas was already a bit worried about Rita, because, on the way over to the restaurant, she briefly had a period of confusion and didn't know where she was. She came out of it, but Silas knew that was probably the beginning of the end.

The clock was ticking, and Silas was very anxious for Sarah and Rita to get to know one another.

Sarah arrived a few minutes after seven and found Rita and Silas sitting outside at a table facing a canal. The canals were the reason why Venice Beach was called Venice Beach, because the founder of the Venice Beach neighborhood, at the turn of the 20th century, envisioned canals that resembled those found in Venice, Italy. Silas was quite sure Sarah was aware of this factoid, her being a former architect, and probably was a student of local history just like himself.

Sarah looked beautiful, of course. She was dressed casually, in black flared pants, a sleeveless button down white shirt, and Espadrilles. She wasn't wearing a lot of makeup, but she was one woman who didn't need it. Silas knew Sarah was the kind of girl who ordinarily would've intimidated Rita. She was the kind of woman who intimidated a lot of women. But Rita felt comfortable with Sarah. That much Silas knew.

Sarah sat down at the table with them. "I have to say, I'm nervous about this situation."

Silas knew why she was worried. Anybody would be in her situation. After all, it wasn't every day a woman tried to get the approval of a current dying wife. And Sarah probably thought that whether or not the two of them went forward all depended on whether or not Rita gave the thumbs-up.

Of course, Silas knew differently. There was really no way Rita could get to know Sarah enough to know whether or not the two of them would go to distance. After all, they were just having one dinner together. A single dinner wouldn't tell Rita enough about Sarah to make a judgment. So Silas knew he probably would go forward with Sarah no matter what Rita said. Still, it was very important to him that Rita like Sarah, because, after all, it was Rita's final wish that she found somebody he could end up happy with. And if Rita liked Sarah, that would mean she possibly could die happy.

Rita put her hand on Sarah's hand and squeezed. "Sarah, don't be nervous. I'm the one who should be nervous of the two of us. After all, I'm the one who's not going to be here in a few days."

The way Rita said that was like she was talking about what she was going to order for dinner. That was still strange for Silas, but, at the same time, it meant his wife had accepted her impending fate and was at peace with it. That obviously made him feel good.

Sarah nodded nervously. "You don't know that," she began.

"Oh, but I do. I know the score here. I'm experiencing terminal lucidity and only 6% of people in this stage of the game survive another week. I'm lucky to be here right now. It's a blessing, really. An absolute blessing."

Silas swallowed hard. He didn't want this dinner to be maudlin or morose. He wanted everything to be light and fun. But maybe that was too much to ask, considering the circumstances.

Sarah just nodded again. She was shaking a tiny bit. Silas felt for her.

"Sarah," Rita said. "I'm sorry to bring the whole atmosphere down. We won't talk anymore about what's about to happen to me. I really want to know more about you."

The waitress came around and took their orders. Sarah

ordered the arugula salad and sashimi. Rita ordered cucumber salad and nothing else. Silas knew why - his wife still couldn't eat heavy food of any kind. That was why this place was perfect - everything on the menu was light and fresh. Silas ordered the Caesar salad Peruvian scallops on the half shell. Amelia ordered the shrimp tempura taco and charred Napa cabbage.

Sarah got a glass of Zinfandel Rosé wine and Silas ordered the Domaine du Pave Tressallier, a French white wine. Sarah smiled.

"You chose a good one there," she said. "I love a good Tressallier."

Rita leaned forward. "What is a Tressallier?" she asked.

Sarah cleared her throat. "It's a bit like a Chablis, but it has some earthy notes, as well as notes of sea salt, citrus and hazelnuts."

"Oh, that sounds amazing. Love hazelnuts and combined with citrus, that sounds like a really interesting combination. Especially if it's a bit salty."

"It is amazing," Sarah said.

"Tell me more about the wine," Rita said. "Tell me everything. This stuff fascinates me."

"Well," Sarah began. "The Tressallier grape is very rare, almost extinct. It comes from the Saint-Pourcain valley of France, which is one of the oldest wine regions in France. It's usually a blended grape, often with a Chardonnay, but this restaurant features a wine made just with that grape. It's bright and brisk, yet subtly rich. It's quite delicious."

Rita's eyes got wide. "Oh, my, you know all that on the top of your head?"

Sarah nodded. "I own a winery and I was a sommelier for my sister when she owned a B&B on Nantucket Island. And I traveled extensively around the world, learning all about wines everywhere I went. I've spent a great deal of time in the French countryside. It's one of my favorite countries."

"What do you like about it?" Rita asked.

"Everything," Sarah said. "The wine, the smells, the food, the people, the beautiful structures that have lasted through world wars, drought, attacks and Mother Nature. It's amazing, really, that anything in France still stands after what happened in both of the world wars." She shook her head. "But that country is so resilient. So magnificent. I love it for those qualities alone."

Silas was seeing why he was so attracted to this woman. It was her passion for life. It was something he could tell the first time he saw her in that café, chatting away with her friends, her smile lighting up the entire room. It was definitely something he could tell when he saw her in action in her winery. It was the way she took care of everybody at her winery, the smile she had for everyone, the relaxed body language she displayed when she was leaning against the winery bar. She was somebody special, he knew, and he was excited to get to know her better.

Then he immediately felt ashamed to feel that way. Rita was still there with them. He had to focus on her.

Rita put her hand on Sarah's arm. "Wow. You really have lived quite a life, haven't you? I never got to leave the country. Well, I went to Mexico a time or two, but I don't know if that counts. I never left North America. Never went overseas." She looked at Silas. "Have you been overseas, Silas?"

Silas took a deep breath. Yes, he had traveled extensively for his curator position. He had been to every continent, even Antarctica. In December of 2006, he traveled to Antarctica with an artist named Xavier Cortada, who traveled to that continent to do various installations and created what Cortada referred to as ice paintings - he used sea ice, glacier and sediment samples and used these to create paintings on canvas.

He had been to Africa to obtain artifacts, installations, sculptures and paintings created by indigenous people. He went to Asia to obtain Hindu and Buddhist sculptures; Chinese bronzes, jades, ceramics and paintings; Japanese screens and woodblock prints; Korean celadon pottery; and Indian and Persian miniature paintings. In Australia, he obtained Aboriginal art, as well as art created by masters living on that continent who were influenced by European modernism. In South America, he traveled extensively to Argentina and Brazil to obtain various surrealist, hyperrealist, and ephemeral art. In Europe, he went to every single country to obtain art.

Yes, he had traveled the world. But Rita didn't know that. She didn't share in these experiences with him, and that made him incredibly sad. Well, she shared in some of them, but she didn't remember those periods of time. Her memory apparently wasn't in those more recent times.

"Yes," he said to Rita. "I've traveled a bit."

She nodded and looked at Sarah. "Tell me about your travels." She blinked rapidly. "I guess your job meant you had to travel, huh?"

Sarah looked uncomfortable. "No," she said slowly and then looked at Silas with a bit of a desperate look in her eyes. Silas didn't know what that look was about, but he recognized the emotions behind this look. Sarah was panicked about something and clearly had some secrets she didn't want to divulge. "I didn't travel for work."

Rita nodded and looked at Silas quizzically. "What

about you, Silas? Where did you go and why did you travel?"

Silas put his arm around Rita protectively. "I traveled for work," he said. "For my curator position. When I was in graduate school, I traveled for various fellowships that enriched my academic credentials and helped me in my doctoral program."

Sarah's face blushed bright scarlet and Silas wondered why.

"Where did you go?" Rita asked Silas. "This is fascinating. I never knew you had wanderlust. I always did, of course, but I never thought you did."

"I didn't have wanderlust when you and I were living on that beach," Silas said. "I didn't have the ambition to go anywhere but to the beach and around the city to get inspiration for my art. It's hard to think about traveling the world when you don't really know where your next meal will come from."

He was avoiding telling Rita about how extensively he had traveled. He didn't want her to know just how much she'd missed out on over the years that she was living in the memory care center. It didn't seem fair, like maybe he was rubbing it in that he had a full life and she didn't.

"Yes," Rita agreed. "When we were living off ham and beans and Ramen noodles, I don't know how we ever could've dreamed of traveling the world. But you've since made something of yourself. Don't be ashamed of that, Silas. I need to know everything you've done over the years. Don't hold back."

Silas looked at Sarah and nodded. "Well," he said, and then told Rita all about his travels. Rita stared in rapt attention as Silas told Rita about going to the African bush and speaking with an African prince who allowed Silas to take several pieces of artwork from his palace; about going to Antarctica with the artist who let him tag along and take photographs of the installations he created in that barren land; about going to China to obtain ancient art from the Ming Dynasty; and all the other places he went to learn about art and obtain art for his curator position.

Sarah, too, was looking at Silas with a look of admiration in her eyes.

"So," Rita said, after Silas talked about his travels in some detail. "It really sounds like you've done quite a bit over the years. Did you learn about wine, too?"

"I did," Silas said. "And I knew this glass of wine would be spectacular." He gestured to the wine, which Rita had took a sip of when he first got it. Rita herself didn't drink much alcohol, so she just got some sparkling water, but she always did enjoy trying whatever Silas ordered. "And it is."

Sarah was quiet while Silas was telling Rita about his travels. It was as if she was holding back because she was ashamed about something. He read her body language and it was screaming that she was embarrassed. He had no idea what that was about.

Rita looked at Sarah. "So, tell me about your travels," she said to Sarah. "I want to live vicariously through you. Tell me everything."

"Well," Sarah said. "There's not much to tell. It was another part of my life that I don't like to think about. It wasn't the happiest period of time."

Rita scrunched her eyebrows. "What do you mean, it wasn't a happy time? You were seeing the world, learning about wines and other cultures and enjoying exotic food. What's not to be happy about?"

Sarah took a deep breath. "Well, my traveling wasn't because I wanted to. It was because, well, I was tied to a man who loved to travel, and I wanted to get away from him as soon as I possibly could." She took a deep breath. "He was an emotionally abusive man who made me feel about two inches tall, but I didn't feel I could leave him because I had no place to go."

Rita nodded and smiled at Silas. She raised an eyebrow at him, and her reaction was clear - she liked Sarah. Sarah had some blemishes, which meant she wasn't the beautiful princess she looked like. She knew hardships, so she could appreciate a man who would cherish her. Silas would be that man to do just that. Rita seemed to now know that Sarah wouldn't be a money-grubbing gold-digger who only wanted to be with him to see how much she could get.

"So, tell me what happened," Rita said. "I don't want to pry and put you on the spot. But I'm curious about your situation with this man."

Then Sarah, after about a pause that lasted forever, told Rita and Silas about Nolan. About how Sarah was forced to take the fall for her "friend" Lauren's drugs, and how Nolan piled on by writing a letter to the California Board of Architects lying about her dealing drugs to children. Sarah explained that Nolan did that to trap her, to ensure she never left him because he was fearing at that time that Sarah was about to do just that. How she hated him but felt like she had no choice but to stay with him because she thought she couldn't find a job or a place to live once she pled guilty to a felony. How she took care of Nolan after he was diagnosed with ALS because she felt it was her obligation.

Rita nodded along. "Wow," she finally said after Sarah told her story. "I was wrong about you. I took one look at you and thought you were like a Barbie doll who had no cares in the world."

Sarah smiled. "Well, if you think Barbie has no cares in the world, you didn't see the movie." And then her face got red right after she said this. "I mean, of course you didn't see that movie. I don't know why I said that."

Rita cocked her head. "No, no, don't worry, Sarah. There was a Barbie movie?"

"Was there," Silas said. "Made over a billion dollars worldwide."

"Really?" Rita said, her eyes getting wide. "A movie about Barbie made that kind of money? Why?"

Sarah shrugged. "I saw the movie, and, I have to confess, I don't really know why it made that much money. I mean, it was a cute movie and it spoke to me, because Ken was irrelevant in the eyes of the main Barbie, and he really is irrelevant in the Barbie world. He always was to me, anyhow. I never really cared about playing with Ken, only with my multitudes of Barbies. And the movie is a bit of a feminist manifesto, where women rule the world and men are just himbo afterthoughts. But, I don't know, it was silly, too. I guess it just hit the zeitgeist because women secretly pine for a world run by females."

Rita laughed and raised her glass and Sarah and she clinked. "You know it, sister," she said. "If women ruled the world, I don't think we'd be in any wars. I think our social safety net would be vastly improved, because women live in a world where the social safety net is necessary. Who can afford child care? And are women still earning seventy cents for every dollar a man earns for the same work?"

"Well, I think it's better now," Sarah said. "Women are more likely to demand what they're worth and I think women own more businesses now than they used to in the past. I think we're all just tired of men having a boot on our necks and we're ready to throw them off."

"So, Thelma and Louise have become a reality these days? I loved that movie, by the way."

"Oh, yes, Thelma and Louise," Sarah said. "I remember watching that movie and fantasizing that I was one of them. They were so free, getting away from their men, letting leches have it, blowing stuff up. In the meantime, I literally had to sneak away to watch that movie. I told Nolan I was having lunch with my idiot friends, when I really was going to the theater to see that movie. It made me cry because it made me feel even more hopeless about my life." She put her hand to her chin. "Actually, now that you bring that movie up, I think I have the answer to why the Barbie movie was so popular. Both the Barbie movie and *Thelma and Louise* represent female wish fulfillment. They both put men in their place. Thelma and Louise paid for sticking it to the man, but Barbie had a good ending."

Silas should've felt intimidated by the conversation the ladies were having about blowing up the patriarchy, but he wasn't. He knew he wasn't like those other toxic men who made women long for a world where women were in power and, in the case of Thelma and Louise, where men were blown away for acting like jerks. Sarah obviously had a terrible experience with an authoritarian asshat who made her feel two inches tall, but he wouldn't ever be like that, so he didn't worry that Sarah was thinking of him when she expressed a longing to put men in their place.

He was confident enough in himself and the way he cherished women to know he was one of the good ones. He wasn't one of the bad ones who made women fantasize about marginalizing men.

Rita put her arm around Silas. "We're talking about feminine wish-fulfillment movies, but, you know, Sarah, not every man acts like that. Silas here has a great love for women. He respects them, loves them. He grew up with a single mother who worked around the clock to give him the world and he worshiped her. But not in a bad way."

Sarah nodded. "I grew up without a father, too," she said. "He died when I was very small. And my mother wasn't the easiest person to be around. Things are great now between myself and my mom, and they always had been okay, if a bit tense. My sister and my mom, though, they always butted heads until recently."

Then Sarah told Rita about her mother's relationship with her long-time love, Violet, and how her mother felt she had to hide who she was for so many years.

"That's so sad," Rita said. "That your mother felt the need to hide for so long."

"Yes," Sarah said. "I agree. And it's tragic that I really didn't get to know Violet that well. I mean, I knew her when I was young, but she wasn't around when I got older. I would've liked to have had her in my life throughout her years, but because my mother didn't want to answer questions about her, I didn't get that chance. Violet died and I didn't even know it until months after it happened."

Sarah shook her head. "Oh, listen, I've been talking and talking. I haven't found out anything about you, Rita. I'm really embarrassed. I don't usually talk this much about myself. Tell me about yourself."

Rita smiled and put her hand on Sarah's arm sympathetically. "Sarah, it's okay. You can find out everything about me from Silas. I really wanted to get to know you. I know Silas is going to be very lonely after I'm gone. All I wanted was to make sure he's going to be looked after when I'm gone. And I have to say, after getting to know you, I think he's going to be just fine."

Silas felt overjoyed to get Rita's stamp of approval, yet

felt ineffably sad at the same time. It was wonderful that Rita approved of Sarah. The sad thing was, as he looked at the two women, he realized that they were becoming friends. And they would've become friends if they would've had the time.

But they didn't have the time. That was the tragedy of the situation.

As the evening wore on, Silas continued to see worrying signs that maybe Rita was leaving her lucid period and was going into her twilight world again. She repeated the exact same story three times in twenty minutes. This was one of the things he noticed about her before she was diagnosed - she repeated the same things over and over again, apparently not remembering she had just told that particular story. She went to the bathroom with Amelia, and, when they sat down, Amelia said Rita was disoriented and forgot where she was.

By the time the evening was over, Silas could see Rita was fading. His heart broke in two as he buckled her into his car, and she looked at him like she didn't know who he was.

Still, he was happy about one thing - Rita met Sarah and Sarah met with her approval.

That meant everything to him.

Chapter Ten

Sarah

Sarah drove away from the dinner with Rita and Silas feeling out of sorts. At first, she and Rita were getting along famously. Like old girlfriends, really. She started to feel as comfortable with the woman as she did with Ava, Quinn and Mia.

But, by the end of the evening, Sarah knew the end was near. And her heart was breaking for the woman. And for Silas.

And, really, for herself. She felt selfish for being so sad about the woman dying, when she didn't really know her. But Rita was such a sweetheart. It just didn't seem fair that she had to go through this at such a young age.

She got home and Quinn was still awake. She and Mia were shooting pool in their new pool room, drinking beer and laughing. It was a Friday night, and the girls were out at the movies with some friends and would be home around 11.

Sarah absolutely adored Mia, Quinn's squeeze. Mia was such a badass and was beautiful, with her assymetrical hair, gorgeous wrinkle-free skin and rocking body that she kept up with three times a week weight training and five days a week bike riding. She'd gotten Quinn involved with bike-riding, too, and the two of them joined riding groups every Saturday morning.

Mia came over to Sarah and put her arm around her. "Hey, Chica," she said. "Wanna play the winner? I can almost guarantee you won't be playing me. Why didn't anybody tell me Quinn was a fucking shark?"

Quinn started to laugh as she walked around the table and sank two balls at once. "Come on, Mia, you give me a run for my money."

Sarah shook her head. Usually, she loved hanging out with the two ladies. But, tonight, she was totally in her head.

Quinn and Mia sensed that. Mia narrowed her eyes and scrunched her nose. "What's up?"

Sarah just shrugged. She was trying to hold back tears and really didn't want to interrupt the happy vibe the two ladies had going on.

"Sugar, what is it?" Quinn asked.

"Oh..." And then Sarah told them about the dinner she had with Rita and Silas.

"Sugar, that's terrible," Quinn said.

Mia nodded. Both women were sitting with Sarah on the couch, one on either side of her. "Sarah, we're here for you," Mia said. "Do you think, uh..."

Sarah nodded. "I don't think she has long left. How can I get involved with Silas? He's going to be grieving her. They've been married for more than 30 years, been together since they were in their teens. And she's been suffering from Alzheimer's for 10 years. I feel guilty even thinking that way."

Quinn and Mia sat there quietly. They looked at one another silently, and Sarah knew something was on their minds.

"What?" Sarah asked. "You guys are thinking something." And she knew that what one was thinking, the other probably was, too. That was how in sync Quinn and Mia were with one another. They could read each other's thoughts. They were almost like Willow, the resident psychic, in that way.

"Well," Quinn began. "It's not the time or place to be saying this, but…"

"I think Quinn wants to say that you shouldn't prejudge the situation," Mia said. "Don't assume Silas will be off-limits after his wife passes. I mean, he might be off-limits at first, but there's something there between you two. Quinn said you were more excited about your date with him than you've been for a long time. That must mean something."

"Yes," Sarah said. "But how shitty am I to be thinking about that? About dating Silas when his wife is in her final days, maybe hours?"

"I'm just saying that you should give him time, but don't forget about him. Fiona said he's your soul mate. Those don't come along every day," Quinn said, putting her hand on Mia's cheek. "I found mine. I want you to find yours, too."

Sarah swallowed hard and then heard Julia and Emerson coming through the door.

"Hey, Mom," Julia said to Sarah. Julia calling her "Mom" was music to her ears. There was a long time when she believed Julia would live with her Aunt Hannah in New York, after Aunt

Hannah took Sarah to court in an effort to take custody of the girl. Hannah won that fight in court, but, in the end, did the right thing when she brought Julia back to live with Sarah.

Hannah and her sister, Mary, were still mending their rift, but were coming along great with that. Hannah funded an art gallery on Gallery Row that featured Mary's paintings and sculptures, and helped Mary sell her paintings online. Mary was becoming a success, all due to Hannah's efforts to market her, and Hannah, for her part, seemed much happier now that she was living by the beach and not working a million hours a week in a law firm. Hannah was even looking into how to become an art agent and publicist, like she was doing for Mary, a second act for her she was very excited about.

"Hey, Jules," Sarah said, putting her arm around her daughter. She had a daughter! That still seemed strange to her. That was all she'd ever wanted in her life, but never managed to have children because Nolan didn't want kids. Then Sarah met Max, a man who was dying of melanoma and wanted Sarah to take Julia after he passed. And now Julia was considered her daughter. The formal adoption was still pending, but it was just a formality. Julia was, for all intents and purposes, Sarah's daughter. And Sarah couldn't be happier about that.

Emerson looked at Sarah. "Hey, Sarah," she said. "What's wrong?"

Emerson was a sensitive sort. For all her bluster and outward bad-assness, she really was the one to dig into what was bothering people. Julia didn't really seem to notice that anything was amiss, but Emerson picked up on it right away.

"Nothing, gorgeous girl," Sarah said. "I'm just tired."

"Calling bs," Emerson said. "But, whatevs. Anyhow, Mom, going to bed."

"Night, night," Quinn said. "How was the movie?"

"Good, I guess," Emerson said. "All those Marvel movies start looking the same, though. Seriously, can't Hollywood come up with something different once in a great while?"

"We liked *Oppenheimer,*" Julia reminded Emerson. "That was different."

"Yeah. Few and far between, though. Few and far between. Anyhow, Mom, see you in the morning."

Julia hugged Sarah, Quinn and Mia, and then followed Emerson upstairs.

"Well," Sarah said. "Like the girls, I'm pretty tired. I'll see you guys in the morning."

At 9 AM, Silas called Sarah.

"Rita passed at 2 this morning," he simply said. "Services will be this Monday at noon at Cathedral of Our Lady of the Angels. I hope you can make it."

Sarah put her hand over her mouth. This was unexpected yet totally expected. She could never get over how every death, no matter how imminent it was, was always simultaneously shocking and expected.

"I'll be there" she said.

She hung up and then sobbed like she hadn't sobbed in a long, long time.

Chapter Eleven

Silas

Silas took a heavy breath as he approached the church where Rita's services were to be held. Rita was a Catholic, through and through, and told Silas that she wanted a good Catholic girl service. So, of course he would give her that.

When he died, he didn't want a religious service at all. He had no use for religion, in general, and saw no need to put on airs about it. He really wanted people to gather at a restaurant or bar and just pass stories around about him. Hopefully the stories would be good. He thought they would be.

He was a little taken aback at how full the church was. He'd put her obituary in the paper, and people apparently flocked to the church to pay their last respects. Rita's younger sister was there. And, of course, there were many people from the memory care place there. Rita was a much loved resident and had been there for so long that she'd made many admirers.

When Silas took Rita home after dinner with Sarah, he knew his wife had little time left. He was grateful that she had a few days of lucidity, where she was his Rita again for only a little while. But when she started to decline, it happened precipitously. Like she went over a cliff and just never came back.

Just then, he saw Sarah coming up the steps. She was by herself and looked stunning in her simple black dress and black pumps. Her blonde hair was swept up in a chignon and her makeup was simple. She looked sad.

He didn't quite know how to react to her. On the one hand, his heart soared when he saw her. Like he saw her and saw his future. Then he immediately felt guilty for feeling so strongly about this woman. He was at his wife's celebration of life service, for the love of God. How could he possibly be looking at somebody else and let his mind go to how ripe her lips looked or how blue her eyes were? How her cheeks were the perfect color of peach, which made him think further about sweetness and light? His mind was supposed to be dark. Was supposed to only be focused on the passing of his wife.

She smiled, shook his hand politely, and he felt awful that he felt a shock of electricity go through him when his hand met hers. "Sarah," he said. "I'm so glad you could make it."

"Of course," she said. "I didn't know Rita for very long, but I really felt a connection with her."

She smiled again and then walked into the church.

Thirty minutes later, Silas was seated at the front of the church and the services began. The priest gave the usual speech about God, Jesus and how Rita was in the bosom of heaven, and then person after person spoke about his wife. Rita touched many lives in the short time she was on this earth, that much was clear. Many of the speakers were people who knew her growing up. Her younger sister talked tearfully about how Rita worked so hard to make sure there was food on the table when her mother was dying and their father was dead. Everybody talked about how kind she was, how good, how loving.

Silas smiled, listening to all the speakers. He loved that his wife touched so many lives. He didn't want to speak, however. He wasn't much of a speaker, and really had no words. He loved his wife, and now she was gone.

The service lasted for the better part of two hours. Rita was cremated so would be put into a niche. There was no need for people to meet at the gravesite. Silas was relieved about that. He remembered his mother's funeral, and how he cried and cried when he saw his mother's casket going into the ground. He always felt his mother literally worked herself to death, as she worked around the clock, it seemed, to make sure he had everything he needed. She worked in a factory, as a waitress, and as a graveyard shift security guard, all at the same time. When did she sleep? So she died at the age of 40, when Silas was 22, which meant she didn't get to see him become the success he eventually became.

And, in the end, Rita also didn't get to see his success. The two people he cared about most in the world never got to see him achieve his dreams, and that was a tragedy in itself.

Sarah had left the service without really finding Silas. Granted, Silas was busy with talking to a multitude of people as a line formed to shake his hand and give them a hug as various people left the church. It seemed like a never ending stream of people wanted to console him, but he felt inconsolable.

And now that Rita had breathed her last, his China trip

was back on. Unfortunately, it couldn't be postponed any longer, because the museum had a firm date for the collection to have its debut, and Silas had to go to China to secure this collection for the museum. He was happy about that and sad at the same time. He was happy because he was fulfilling the terms of his contract for this particular collection. He was sad because he felt empty now. Like a part of him was gone for good. What would he do with himself now that Rita was gone? All those afternoons he went to visit her at the memory care center would be no more. There would be no more chatting with Amelia, no more holding Rita's hand. Even though she never knew who he was, it was still comforting for him to be there with her.

He drove home to his empty house. The house was, to be sure, always empty before, save for Silas himself. Rita was never able to live in that house with him. But the house never seemed as empty and barren as it did that day. It was just that the presence of Rita, which he always felt around this house even though she was some 10 miles away at the memory care place, was now gone. And he realized just how meaningless his home really was. It was beautiful, right on the beach, a symbol of his success. But it was just not him. Not really.

And, on the spur of the moment, he decided to call a real estate agent to sell this place. Maybe while he was gone in China, his real estate agent, Stacy, could get this place sold.

But then he got into his car, and didn't call Stacy.

He called Sarah.

Chapter Twelve

Sarah

Sarah left Rita's services feeling devastated. She hated funerals. Nobody really liked them, but Sarah remembered, all too well, her father's funeral all those years ago. She was very young, only around five years old, but she understood everything going on around her. And she understood just how tragic her father's early death was.

She got home, made herself a sandwich, and went to Julia's room to see what she was up to. Julia was sitting on her bed, reading a book, which was what she usually did when she was not baking, hanging out with Emerson, or writing a song.

"Hey, kid," Sarah said to Julia. "What's going on?"

Julia shrugged. "Just reading a book about *The Summer I turned Pretty*," she said. "I'm going to start the series on Netflix, so I wanted to read the book first. How are you?"

"I'm sad. I'm sad for Silas. I don't know him, but yet I feel I really do. I know it doesn't make any sense."

"Do you think he might be The One?" Julia asked. Julia loved their living arrangement. Sarah, Quinn, Emerson and Julia lived under the same roof. Julia didn't say as much, but Sarah knew that if something happened, and Sarah met a man and got married, they would have to move out of this house and into another. Sarah knew Julia would not be happy about that. She was as close as a sister to Emerson, and Sarah knew it meant a lot to Julia to be around her best friend all the time. Not to mention the fact that Julia was very close with Quinn and Mia as well.

Sarah laughed. "It's a little soon for that. I do like him though. I think he's a good man."

Sarah didn't want to go into the specifics of why she thought Silas was a good man. She didn't want to tell Julia all about the convoluted situation between Silas, Rita, and herself. She didn't want to admit to Julia that, ironically enough, she felt Silas was a good man because of the tender way he treated his wife. She certainly didn't want to encourage Julia to think she was going after a married man. And she really wasn't. She was definitely going to give him space.

Just then, her phone rang.

It was Silas.

"Hey," she said. "How are you?"

"I'm at the beach," he said, not really answering her question. "I'm going to China for real tomorrow. And I was wondering if I could see you."

"Which beach?"

"I live on a private beach. Let me give you my address. I was hoping maybe you could meet me here. Not at my house, but on the beach by my house."

"Sure." Sarah got out a pen and paper, and wrote down the address.

Twenty minutes later, Sarah approached Silas. Once again, like she saw him before from afar, he was standing at the edge of the water, his hands stuck in his pockets.

When she got close to him, she saw he had tears in his eyes. He smiled ruefully, and put his arm around her. "Glad you could make it," he said.

"Of course," Sarah said. But she stood there silently next to him, because she didn't know what else to say. She would just let him talk.

"Sarah," he began. "What can I say? I felt struck by lightning the first time I saw you. But that's not why I called you to come today."

"I understand," Sarah said slowly.

"Maybe you do. Maybe you don't. Anyhow, I'm in a confused state right now. My best friend, the woman I thought I would spend my life with, has died and I feel adrift." He paused and looked at the rolling ocean. "I really thought you and I could make a go of it. But I don't know now. I didn't anticipate I'd feel this pain, this hole in my heart."

Sarah just nodded. "I think I know what you're trying to say. I think you probably need a lot of time to deal with this."

"Yes. I am going to China for 10 days, starting tomorrow. I really hope I can get a handle on things while I'm there. I'm not making any promises, of course. How can I make promises to you right now? I guess I just wanted to say thank you for coming to Rita's service today. Thank you for meeting with Rita and me the other night. I think you made her last few hours happy. She really wanted to know I would be okay."

"Are you going to be okay?"

He shook his head. "I don't even know what okay is

anymore. I've known Rita for so long, I just can't imagine a world without her. I know that's not what you want to hear, and that's not really what I wanted to say, either. I'm just playing things minute by minute."

Sarah stood next to him, looking at the water and hearing the waves come in. She knew it was quite possible this would be the last time she'd see this man. She didn't know what it was like to lose someone she romantically loved. She lost Nolan, but she didn't love Nolan, so it wasn't the same. She didn't know what this guy was going through, but it was obvious he was devastated.

"I understand. And I'll be around whenever you are ready. I'm not going anywhere. And you know where to find me."

He chuckled a little. "Yeah, I do know where to find you."

At that, Sarah just put her arm around him, squeezed, and left.

She didn't know where they stood.

She only knew that she was at Silas's mercy.

That didn't feel good at all.

Chapter Thirteen

Sarah

Seven months later

Over the next few months, Sarah went about her business and tried to put Silas out of her mind. It wasn't all that difficult to do for her. After all, she barely knew him. Fiona's insistence that the two of them were meant to be together notwithstanding, Sarah knew that, while she and Silas had a connection, it wasn't strong enough of a connection to survive what happened between Silas and his wife Rita.

And she had to be realistic. Things probably were not going to work out with her and Silas. In the meantime, she was turning down offers to go out from eligible men, left and right. She was used to men asking her out all the time. But it really was something that happened a lot now that Sarah was part owner of a winery and came in contact with many handsome and eligible men around her age.

She was still hanging out with her friends who were all in relationships, but, at the moment, Sarah didn't want to join them in their happily ever after status. She started to not mind going out with Ava and Elijah. That was because Ava and Elijah apparently got through their infatuation stage, where they were PDA all over town, and got to the stage where the initial sex-fueled glow was cast aside for a much more comfortable feeling. Sarah knew Ava and Elijah were built to go the distance, so it was inevitable that they would move into the more mature phase of the relationship, and so they were. So it was much less uncomfortable for Sarah to go out with the two of them.

The same dynamic was happening with Hallie and Conrad. So, even when she went out with her ladies for dinner, and their respective beaus - Ava, Elijah, Hallie, Conrad, Quinn and Mia - she didn't necessarily feel like an extra wheel to the whole group. Everybody just talked and laughed like friends, and nobody acted in a way that made Sarah feel like she was an outsider. So things were going well with her friend group as far as that went.

But she was feeling the pull of wanting to hook up with somebody. So, one Saturday night in early October, when the crisp fall air was just beginning and Sarah was looking forward to the time change when dusk would fall at around 4 PM and soon there would be trick-or-treaters coming to their door, she accepted a date with a man by the name of Matthew Connelly.

Matthew was a very handsome guy and played center for the Los Angeles Kings, the NHL hockey team. Sarah knew little about him or about the Kings, in general, but he seemed to be a fun guy and was definitely interested in Sarah, so she decided to give it a go.

She really decided to give him a try because he was so

sweet about it. He had been to her winery five separate times before he finally asked her out. He told her the reason he kept coming around was because he really wanted to ask her out, but felt intimidated by her so he never could do it the previous times he was there at the winery. Sarah actually found that charming, that an NHL player would be shy about asking out a woman. She had read enough romance novels about NHL players that made her believe that they all were man-whores going after puck bunnies, but this guy seemed to not be.

Still, he was quite a bit younger than her. He told Sarah he was 35. She was 54, so almost 20 years older than him. Not that that was a deal-breaker, necessarily, but Sarah always preferred to go out with men who had similar touchstones as herself. She remembered the days when she would watch MTV religiously for their videos, and could name all the original MTV VJs. She came of age when the second British Invasion hit the shores, as one cool English band after another made the music of her youth, Duran Duran being her favorite. He came of age in the early 2000s. Sarah couldn't really remember the music that was popular during that time, which told her everything. Still, they both loved the bands Weezer and Green Day, music that was popular when Sarah was in her 20s and Matthew was a toddler. That wasn't surprising for Sarah, though - she went to a concert featuring Green Day, Weezer and Fall Out Boy, and found most of the audience was in their 20s. So, the younger generation appreciated good music, too, which was heartening. She found the same thing at a Duran Duran concert - that band also appeared to appeal to the young.

More than that, she remembered 9/11. She knew just where she was when she heard about that. Matthew did, too, but he was a small child, only 12 years old, so he experienced it much differently than she did.

That was all silly stuff, in the end, Sarah thought. Still, she assumed that if she started seeing Matthew, it wouldn't amount to much of anything. She only said yes to a date because she was sick of turning everyone down and finally decided that Silas and her were not meant to be.

Ava had a good time ribbing Sarah about her impending date. "Wow, an NHL star, huh, Sarah? I always knew you would end up dating the star athlete. Surprised you never did in high school."

And that was true. Sarah might've been the most popular girl in school, but she loved the artsy nerds even in high school. Everybody wanted her to date the captain of the football team, Bruce Warner, and Bruce was certainly interested, but Sarah dated guys like Vincent Daniels, who was an artist and a member of the chess club, and Nick Wallace, a bookish guy who was on the yearbook staff and was a photographer. Even then, Sarah didn't go in for the lunkheads.

Not that all athletes were lunkheads, necessarily. There were plenty of football players in high school who made the honor roll, or played an instrument in band, or were in the chess club. But Sarah steered clear of the athletes, nonetheless, even though those athletes were the natural fit for her.

Now she was going to apparently date an athlete. Not just any athlete, but a professional one. How strange was that?

She sighed. "Yes, Ava, I guess I am finally going to date the jock that everyone thought I should back in the day."

She and Ava were drinking wine at their winery. Hallie was going to join them later on, because Hallie was still working at the retreat that was also in the Santa Monica Mountains and she often stopped by after she got off work. It was important that at least one person was perfectly sober to drive down the mountain, and Hallie would be that person. Ava and Sarah would leave their cars at the winery and Hallie would drive them home. Then they would Uber to their cars the next day.

As for who was tending the winery, it was Aria, the girl they hired as a wine tender, along with Oliver, a UCLA student who worked part-time. Both Aria and Oliver were in their twenties and were anxious to learn about wine for different reasons - Aria was working on a culinary degree at the The Chef Apprentice School of the Arts on Wilshire Boulevard and Oliver was working on a hospitality management certification at UCLA. They both loved working at the Sava winery and said they were learning a lot.

Sarah sipped her wine and looked at the sky. It was so odd, really. Not a day went by that she didn't think about Silas. About what he was doing, how he was holding up, and whether he thought about her. He hadn't contacted her in all these months, though. Sarah wasn't going to reach out to him, either. She felt the ball was in his court. He was the one going through the grieving of his wife. He was the one who told Sarah, in so many words, to back off because he needed space. Sarah wanted to contact him, every day. But she didn't want to be a pest. Somehow, she thought she would be if she tried to talk to him.

Ava thought Sarah was make a mistake with Silas. That much was clear. Ava thought that Sarah should go ahead and make the first move, if only to see how Silas was doing. If only to show her support for what Silas was going through. And Sarah knew she should do that. That would be the kind thing to do. But she couldn't shake the feeling that she would just be intruding. That she would just be rushing things that clearly couldn't be rushed.

Ava wasn't the only one upset with Sarah for not contacting Silas. Fiona was, too. Fiona told Sarah just about every time she saw her that Silas was meant to be hers. Fiona kept telling Sarah that Silas was her soulmate.

But, no matter how much Ava, Fiona, and, for that matter, Quinn, Mia and Hallie, told Sarah that she needed to reach out to Silas, Sarah never did.

So, here she was, making a date with an NHL star, just because she was tired of not dating anybody when all of her friends were matched up. She certainly wasn't going out with Matthew because she felt any great connection to him.

Sarah wrapped her pashmina closer around her shoulders. It was getting just a bit chilly, as it tended to do in Southern California during fall crisp evenings. She knew Ava was wanting to give her a lecture about dating a puppy like Matthew when she could have somebody who really got her, like Silas. She didn't want to hear it, and Ava knew it, so they were just going to talk around it. Like they did.

"Well, I hope you have fun."

Sarah rolled her eyes. "Yeah, fun. I'm sure I'll have fun with a guy who is easily recognizable and probably has people coming up to him all the time asking for his autograph. I'm sure I'll have fun with a guy who's attractive to tons of nubile twenty-somethings who have much more in common with him than I ever will."

Sarah did a little bit of Googling of the guy. Got on his Wikipedia page. She was hoping to see a glimmer of something of substance in this guy, some kind touchstone that would make her believe they would have anything to talk about at all. Maybe he had some secret hobby, some kind of artistic or musical bent, or, like Brad Pitt, maybe was interested in architecture. She remembered reading that about Brad Pitt one time, that he was an architectural buff. In fact, that was Brad Pitt's earlier dream - to become an architect. So, knowing that many talented people had hidden dreams and desires, Sarah hoped that Matthew would be similar.

But she didn't see anything on this page that would tell her he had any of these leanings. Not that that meant he didn't have an interest in the same things she did. It was just that, if he did, it wasn't immediately obvious.

Ava leaned forward. "Sarah, you're not into this. You are going out with a guy who you have nothing in common with, just because he happened to ask you out when you're sick and tired of being alone. And, somewhere out there, in Malibu, there is a man who's right for you."

Sarah sighed. "You see, Ava, here's the thing. I met him when he was married. And his wife was dying at the time. I don't know if I can get past that. The guilt of knowing I'm only with a man because his wife got a cruel disease and died way before her time. A man who I became infatuated with during her final days. It's just not sitting right with me. I really wish he would have come to me when he didn't have those set of facts."

What Sarah was trying to say, in the most artful way possible, was that she wished Silas would have only contacted her after Rita had passed away. That if that were the case, she obviously would not feel this sense of guilt she felt about stepping on poor Rita's toes when Rita was virtually on her death bed.

"Sarah," Ava said. "I know you. I'm your sister. You're making excuses. You just don't want your heart broken again."

"Quit trying to psychoanalyze me," Sarah said, even though she knew Ava was absolutely correct. Sarah was terrified of getting her heart stomped on again. And she knew a man like Silas, who she seemed to have so much in common with and who gave her more butterflies than she'd ever experience in her life, would do her in if something happened and it all fell apart. So, yes, she was scared. Leave it to Ava to figure that out and call her on it.

"I'm not trying to psychoanalyze you, I'm trying to be a friend. And a loving sister. I just don't want you to settle."

"I'm not settling. I'm going out with this guy and having some fun. That's all. Nothing more, nothing less."

Ava shook her head. "Another thing I know about you, Sarah, is that you would much rather be at home, hanging out with Julia and Emerson than going out with somebody who isn't absolutely right for you."

Ava was right again. Sarah did love hanging out with Julia and Emerson. She loved being a mother to Julia and a virtual mother to Emerson, same as Quinn loved being a mother to Emerson and a virtual mother to Julia. She loved those two girls with all her heart. And she was so looking forward to teaching them and hopefully influencing them not to make the same mistakes she did along the way. She needed to make sure that neither of them got involved in a toxic relationship like she did for so many years.

Not that either of them would get involved with a man like Nolan. Emerson was a genius, the smartest human being that Sarah had ever known. And Julia, while not quite the genius Emerson was, was also very intelligent, and had such a sweet and soft demeanor that she was drawn to the shy types.

Still, Sarah knew that she herself was drawn to the same types of artsy nerds that Julia tended to date, and she still was sucked in by a guy like Nolan. Which meant Julia was not safe from possibly repeating Sarah's mistake, so Sarah really bent over backwards, having talks with Julia and Emerson about life and men, to the point that Emerson rolled her eyes. Emerson was very worldly in her views on dating and boys. Julia was less so, so Sarah still thought she could influence her daughter.

The upshot was, Sarah really didn't want to spend time with anybody who wasn't going to bring something to her life. Her life is too busy to settle. So, why was she settling? She didn't really know. She only knew she'd agreed to a date with Matthew, so she was going through with it.

"Yes, I know," Sarah said. "And, I probably won't go on another date with this Matthew guy. I'm sure it'll just be a one and done. I don't have to commit to him. I'm not marrying the guy. Just one date."

"Okay. I got your message, loud and clear. You're not going to call the person you're supposed to be with. As I said before, have fun."

"We will."

And the topic was closed.

Chapter Fourteen

Silas

Silas was surprised how deeply he went into a depression after Rita passed away. He had his position as an art curator, both for the Los Angeles museum and for various independent art galleries around the Los Angeles area. He was doing his own artwork on the side, just like he was before. He was still making videos of him playing the piano for his YouTube channel.

In short, he was going about his business, like he did while Rita was in the memory care place. Everything should've been exactly the same as it was before, but it wasn't. Rita was no longer in this world, and that cut him deep.

But what cut him even deeper was the fact that he virtually fell in love with Sarah while Rita was still alive. Because Silas now knew that love at first sight was a thing, and he experienced it with Sarah.

He used to think plays like *Romeo and Juliet* and the

updated version, *West Side Story*, were ridiculous at best. How does that happen that you see somebody across a crowded room, and instantly fall head over heels? He didn't think it was possible. Love didn't work like that. Love was something he had with Rita, where he got to know her and admired her for her talent, drive and desire to support her family. He didn't fall in love with Rita at first sight. No, he went to her art booth on the beach, time and again, asking her about her paintings and her inspiration for them. They talked all the time as friends before he decided to ask her out.

Then, after he asked her out, they bonded over their shared love of art and sushi. It was a gradual thing, not at all the bolt of lightning he felt when he saw Sarah, so he trusted it.

He didn't trust his feelings for Sarah. He didn't think they could be so strong for someone he didn't know. But, more than that, he felt incredibly guilty for feeling that strongly for Sarah while his wife was dying. What kind of person was he? What kind of person could he be when he fell in love with somebody else while his wife was in a memory care center, in the final stages of a horrible disease? He wasn't a good person at all, certainly wasn't good enough for someone like Sarah.

So, he decided to just put his feelings for Sarah aside and try to forget about her.

He also made changes in his life that made him feel better about himself. The first thing was, he sold the huge empty home he lived in on the beach. He realized it was just a big empty place where he felt a keen sense of loneliness and isolation. He decided to buy a much smaller house on a different beach in Malibu. It was just a cottage, really, compared to his giant other home, although most people would think this home was grand as well. He loved it, because it felt homey to him, cozy, with a wood-burning fireplace and a deck that abutted the beach. It had the kind of interior decorating details he loved, from the wood beams on the ceilings, the loft master bedroom, the open floor plan, and the spacious kitchen. It wasn't cold and steel like his last place, but was made of bricks and was Tudor style.

Most important, he now had neighbors. His new house wasn't isolated like his old one, but was part of a row of houses that abutted the same beach. He had next-door neighbors on both sides, so he was friendly with them and didn't feel so alone.

And another thing he decided to do was to get back to basics with his painting. He was going through a period of painting abstract art, and it was extremely popular with the NFT crowd. But it really wasn't meaning much to him anymore, as he used to paint people, landscapes and crowds. He used to capture the vibrancy of the city with his paintings, or the blush of first love, or the passion of ballerinas and musicians and actors. He used to just capture *life* in his paintings. He lost that when he went more abstract. His current art was much more personal to him, and it sold just as well with the NFT crowd, so he decided to keep with it.

And he found himself painting Rita all the time. It helped him whenever he felt the hole in his heart left by her passing.

Then, one day, his oldest friend got into contact with him. Noah White and he grew up together, but Noah had moved to New York City a few years back. They still kept in touch all the time by phone and Zoom, and Noah really wanted to attend Rita's funeral when it happened but was busy with a trip overseas. Noah was a finance guy, looking for businesses to fund, so he traveled as much as Silas did. He was married to a woman named Suzy, and their relationship was much like Silas' with Rita - they met as teenagers and had been in love ever since.

Noah and Suzy were moving to Los Angeles, and Silas was the first person he called about it. Silas was very excited about them coming to town. Maybe having Noah around would cut into his loneliness just a bit. Maybe Noah could bring some life to Silas' dark world.

"Can't wait to see you buddy," Silas said. "When are you coming?"

"In a couple of days. We're moving across the country, and don't want to bother with moving all our stuff. So we're going to pack all the really personal things, but, for the big stuff, we'll buy everything new. But let's have some dinner, like old times. Just you and me, since Suzy will be coming next week. She has to wrap some stuff up at her law office."

Silas smiled and laughed, maybe for the first time in months. He was going to see an old friend, and that was going to be something to look forward to.

Finally.

Chapter Fifteen

Sarah

Sarah and Matthew went to Moonshadows Malibu, an upscale eatery on the beach. The place specialized in seafood, and Sarah loved the vibe of eating on a deck at night and hearing the ocean waves coming in. It was a Friday night, so completely crowded, and she found herself actually having not too bad of a time. Once she got over her initial snobbery about dating a man who had no interest in architecture, art, classical music, traveling or anything Sarah was interested in, and decided to just sit back and have some fun, she found herself doing just that.

Having fun.

The place was packed with people on the deck, the ocean raging below the cliff the restaurant sat on. Matthew turned out to be a very nice guy, a perfect gentleman who opened her car door, brought her roses, and pulled out her chair at the restaurant. Yes, he didn't appear to be her soul mate. But he was handsome, charming, and seemingly very much into her, despite their age difference.

He was also quite popular, as one person after another came to their table to ask for his autograph or congratulate him for the previous night's game. Sarah didn't mind, even the nubile young girls who came up to flirt with him right in front of her. She actually found it humorous, although he seemed embarrassed by all the attention.

"So, Sarah, tell me more about yourself," he said. She had asked him question after question about his hockey career, his college interests, his upbringing, things like that. And now, apparently he wanted to turn the tables and find out more about her.

Oh, that was always a tricky business, trying to tell a new person about her past. She was still so ashamed about it. So, she just gave him the information she wanted to give him, and nothing more.

"Well, as you know, I own a winery, and it's doing very well. I live with my adopted daughter, Julia, her best friend Emerson, and one of my best friends, Quinn and her significant other, Mia." There, that should do it. No need to go into all the messy business about Nolan and about how he trapped her into a relationship.

He nodded. "That's good, but tell me more about yourself," he said. "Where did you go to school, where did you grow up, you know, that kind of thing."

She raised an eyebrow. Again, it was tricky. She was going to tell him about getting a Master's in architecture, but thought better of it. He would inevitably ask her about why she didn't pursue a career in architecture if she had the passion to get a Master's in the field, and that would open a whole can of worms.

It was then that she realized Matthew just wasn't The

One. It seemed to her that if she was sitting across the table from a guy who she was ashamed to be herself around, he wasn't right. She just had a feeling that if she told him everything, he would judge her.

And that was unlike Silas, who was sitting right there when she told Rita about her past with Nolan, and he didn't judge her at all. What's more, she felt comfortable revealing these things about herself to Silas and Rita. She was holding her tongue with this guy, and she didn't know exactly why she was, except she felt in her gut that her story would not be well-received.

She opened her mouth to say a few words of BS to Matthew when she looked across the restaurant and saw the one person she was craving.

Silas was there with a guy about his age. He hadn't yet seen her, but it was just a matter time before he did.

Was this really the reason she decided to go out with Matthew? Because fate had to put her in the same path as Silas that evening? She was a believer in fate, even if she didn't want to always admit that fact. And she couldn't help but think this was fate throwing her together with this man.

Just then, he did catch her eye, and he smiled.

The smile lit her up from within, and she knew.

He really was the man she was supposed to be with. She was running from it, because she was scared. But fate didn't want her running from it, that much was clear.

But she was on a date, so she couldn't do anything about it.

But maybe she could if she could excuse herself to go to the bathroom.

"I'll be right back," Sarah said to Matthew.

Then she got up, took a deep breath, and headed over to Silas' table.

Chapter Sixteen

Silas

Silas was so happy to see Noah. It was such a comfort level to be with his old friend. Like putting on a really old pair of shoes. And, after losing Rita, he really needed the comfort of somebody who really understood and cared about him.

Noah came to Silas' house with a six pack of beer, and the two men sat on Silas' deck around a fire pit, reminiscing about old times and laughing. They went way back, because Noah knew Silas when he lived in the van on the beach. And he knew Rita very well.

The topic soon came to Silas and Sarah. It was brought up when Noah asked Silas about how he was holding up after Rita's death, and whether he could ever see himself moving on.

"Well, here's the thing." Silas felt comfortable talking to Noah about his feelings for Sarah, because he knew his old friend would not judge him for feeling strongly about somebody so soon after his wife's death. "I did meet somebody special. Right before Rita passed."

Noah nodded. He could read his friend's mind. "Silas, that was bad timing. Nothing more. Where is this woman now?"

"I don't know," Silas admitted. "I haven't been in contact with her since Rita's celebration of life."

Noah put his hand on Silas' shoulder. "Buddy," he said, "here's the thing. I know you're racked with guilt, but you shouldn't be. It couldn't be helped what happened with Rita. And I'm sure she wanted you to be happy."

"Yes," Silas said. "She wanted me to be happy. That's why she wanted to meet Sarah."

Noah raised an eyebrow. "Meet Sarah. How did she know about her?"

Then Silas explained all about his confessing his feelings for Sarah to Rita, and Rita meeting Sarah at dinner. "She really liked Sarah," Silas said.

Noah shook his head. "Okay," he said. "Now I know you need to get off your pity pot. What kind of respect are you showing for Rita's last wish? Do you think she's looking down at you right now and feeling happy? Or pissed that you're not moving on like she wanted you to?"

Silas knew the answer to that one. Rita, wherever she was, probably *was* pissed at him for giving Sarah the cold shoulder. She was somewhere wondering what the hell was wrong with him.

"She's mad, I'm sure," Silas said. "But I can't help how I feel. I shouldn't have fallen in love with somebody else while my wife was suffering in a memory care center. I was unfaithful in my heart and I can't get past that."

Noah leaned forward and took a stick to poke around the rocks in the fire pit, then shook his head. "Silas, man, you deserve happiness. I know you have some survivor's guilt about Rita dying and you living. But, trust me, your choice to not live your life, to just wait around to die instead of living, isn't doing anybody any favors."

Silas knew this. Intellectually, he knew everything Noah was telling him was true. But emotionally, he just couldn't bring himself to acknowledge how he was doing. He'd thrown himself into his work, and moving from one house to another took weeks. Since his new house was so much smaller than his last one, he had to sell much of his furniture and fixtures in the house, and put much of it in storage. So, his work and his moving took most of his emotional energy over the last few months, and, he had to admit, he was looking for another outlet for his energies.

Another outlet that didn't involve love. Because Noah was right - he didn't feel right about moving on. Maybe he did have survivor's guilt about the whole thing. He felt he didn't deserve a full life because Rita didn't get to have the same.

Noah was holding a mirror to his face and he wasn't liking what he saw.

Silas swallowed hard. "Let's change the subject. Better yet, let's grab something to eat."

"Sure," Noah said. "What are you in the mood for?"

"Seafood," Silas said. "Moonshadows Malibu." He blurted out the name of that restaurant even though he hadn't been thinking about it before. But there was some reason why he really, really wanted to go there that evening. Something was pulling him in that direction.

He shook his head. What was this? This thinking that Rita was up there somewhere, guiding him along in his life? Because that was what he thought about when he said the words "Moonshadows Malibu" - he was thinking about his wife. It was almost like she was whispering in his ear about that restaurant.

"That sounds good," Noah said. "I love that place myself."

"I do too," Silas said. "But that's not why I want to go there."

"Oh? Why do you want to go there?"

Silas shrugged. "I don't really know. I just have a feeling something good will happen there."

"Okay, let's go," Noah said. "I'm starving. I could eat a whole swordfish at this point."

Silas scrunched his nose. "Swordfish isn't my favorite. I like the light stuff, like Swai, Tilapia, Roughy and Cod."

"To each his own," Noah said. "Let me give a quick call to Suzy, and we'll get going."

"Call her in the car," Silas said and then shook his head. What was the rush? He didn't know. He only knew he needed to be at that place as soon as possible.

"Will do," Noah said.

Then the two men hopped into Silas' Range Rover. Noah talked to Suzy on the way there.

Silas was anxious to get there.

He looked up through his moonroof and spoke aloud while his friend was talking to the love of his life. "Rita, are you there? Give me a sign."

He turned on the radio and got his sign.

Their song, Bonnie Tyler's *Total Eclipse of the Heart* was playing. That was the song that was all the rage when the two met, when Rita was 16 and he was 18. They fell in love listening to this song on his radio as they parked by the beach, looking at the stars through the moonroof of his 1975 Trans AM, a blanket on both of them and poetry uttering through his lips to her.

They decided that night that that song was their song. He hadn't heard it in years, although he always loved it. It was such an anthem, really, a big song that some people thought cheesy but was a song he loved from the very beginning. So did Rita.

"Turn around bright eyes," he said dreamily. He was now in the parking lot of the restaurant, and he closed his eyes. Who was the bright eyes, now? Rita or Sarah?

As he closed his eyes, he got his answer.

Sarah came into view, not Rita.

It was time to move on.

"Thanks, babe," he said softly, looking through the moon roof. "I'll see you again, but thanks for giving me your blessing."

Noah got off the phone. "Well, we're here," he said. "Let's go."

Chapter Seventeen

Sarah

Sarah's heart was pounding out of her chest and her legs felt weak as she approached Silas' table. She had no idea how she would be received. After all, the guy hadn't contacted her in over six months. No texts, no emails, no calls, no Facebook messages. No nothing.

Wasn't that her answer? He didn't want to see her or talk to her. So why was she walking over to his table? Wasn't she intruding? The only thing that ameliorated the situation was that he wasn't on a date.

Silas stood up as she approached him. "Sarah," he said, and then he wrapped his arms around her. He held her for a long time, his face in her hair as if he was inhaling her scent. "This is why I'm here."

They finally parted and Silas was looking at the sky and smiling and nodding. Sarah didn't know what that was about, but she was relieved that he seemed happy to see her.

The man with Silas stood up, too, looking at Sarah questioningly.

"Oh, yes," Silas said. "I'm so sorry, Sarah, where's my head? Sarah, this is Noah, my oldest friend. Noah, Sarah."

Noah smiled and shook Sarah's hand. "Good to meet you." Then he nudged Silas. "I think Sarah's on a date with Matthew Connelly, the Kings' center."

Silas looked over at the table where Sarah was sitting and saw poor Matthew sitting there, drinking a glass of wine and clearly wondering where Sarah went off to.

Sarah felt awful for being there with Matthew. The poor man certainly liked her and, thus far, had treated her like a queen. Sarah was standing there, wanting, more than anything, to go down to the beach with Silas. She pictured herself taking her shoes off and letting the ocean waves lap at the bottom of her black pants, feeling the warm sand squish between her toes as she walked, hand in hand, with this man who she was magnetically attracted to.

But she couldn't. That would be beyond bad for her to do that. Sarah was, if nothing else, a polite person. She was also somebody who hated to hurt anyone. Yet, as she looked into Silas' green eyes, she realized that, if Matthew was liking her and wanting to see her again, she would have to hurt him.

Because she finally realized that Silas was The One. As crazy as that was in her head, that she saw her future in the eyes of a man she knew for not even a week and hadn't communicated with for the past six months, she really did believe that Silas was her person.

Maybe fate was smiling at her and Silas, though, because she looked back at Matthew and saw a woman sitting at the table in her place. She raised an eyebrow and patted Silas' cheek. "I have a feeling I'll be right back," she said.

She walked over to her table, and Matthew stood up. "Sarah," he said. "Um…"

The woman at the table looked at Sarah and Sarah suddenly understood. The woman's name was Naomi White, and Sarah recognized her as Matthew's longtime girlfriend. They'd recently broken up, or so the gossip went. Sarah knew all this because she did her research on Matthew and found out everything about him before the date.

"Hello," Naomi said sweetly to Sarah. "I better get back to my girlfriends. Matthew, it was good to see you."

He nodded, his face flushing scarlet.

He gestured to the chair across from him, the chair that Sarah was sitting in. Sarah cocked her head as she sat down, and took a sip of her wine.

"Matthew," Sarah said. "Did you know Naomi would be here tonight?"

"Yes," he said, clearly embarrassed. "I saw that info on her Facebook page."

Sarah had to stifle a laugh. "Matthew, dear, I'm surprised you would invite me out to dinner with you. If you wanted to make your ex-girlfriend jealous, you probably should've invited somebody more your age."

Matthew looked down at his own glass of wine, clearly busted. "Sarah, that's not why I invited you out," he tried to say.

"It is, but that's okay." Then she looked over at Naomi, who was with her friends, but staring at Matthew intently. "Go. She's clearly still in love with you, and, I dare say, you feel the same about her."

He scrunched his brows. "Really? You aren't pissed?"

"Who am I to stand in the way of young love?" Sarah asked rhetorically. Matthew wasn't all that young - he was 35 - but, to her, he was positively a zygote. And not at all what she was looking for.

He left a bunch of cash on the table to pay for the meals - he left a generous $150 tip, Sarah noticed with admiration - kissed Sarah on the cheek and went to find Naomi.

Sarah smiled as Naomi got out of her seat when Matthew approached, and the two of them went into the restaurant, and, presumably, out to Matthew's car to have wild make-up sex. Or, at least, Sarah hoped that was about to happen.

Everybody deserved to be with their person, Sarah thought. Yes, Matthew apparently used her to make his ex-girlfriend jealous, but so what? She was using him, too, in a way. She used him as a buffer against being alone.

Just then, Silas approached. "Sarah, can I sit down?" he asked.

"Of course," Sarah said, feeling butterflies. Her heart seemed to skip a million beats as Silas sat down across from her. She leaned forward and sighed. "How have you been?"

"Well, it's been rough," he said. "But I think I'm through the worst." He looked down at the beach below. "It's a cool night," he said. "But I love a good beach walk. Are you up for it?"

Sarah got her pashmina, that was laid on the back of her chair, and wrapped it around her. "Let's go," she said. "Is your friend okay with your leaving?"

"He is," Silas said. "To say the least." He looked shy. "Noah really wants me to move on. He loved Rita, but she's gone. And he reminded me that Rita wanted nothing but happiness for me. Not the dark place I've been living in for the past six months."

The two of them went into the restaurant and walked out the front door. Sarah smiled as she saw Matthew and Naomi a bit further in the parking lot, holding hands and walking slowly to Matthew's car.

Sarah and Silas walked down to the beach. Silas rolled up the bottom of his pants and Sarah did the same. Then Silas took Sarah's hand and the two of them stood in the sand, the waves coming in and lapping around their ankles. The moon was full and the tide was high, the whooshing sound of wave after wave in Sarah's ears.

"Sarah," Silas said. "I've thought about you constantly for the past few months. Then I'd feel guilty for thinking about you so much, so I would actively try to put you out of my mind. That's why I haven't contacted you. I felt a duty to Rita to keep her as my number one lady."

Sarah nodded. She understood. Not from personal experience, but by talking with her mother. Her mother lost the love of her life, Violet, in a sudden way. Her mother confessed to Sarah that she felt guilty for wanting to date somebody new. Like it would be a betrayal to Violet. She finally figured out that life was for the living, and was now engaged to a woman named Barbara.

Apparently, Silas felt the same. That he would be betraying Rita's memory if he moved on with Sarah.

"How do you feel now?" Sarah asked.

Silas looked up at the moon, the water lapping around his legs. His shirt was slightly open, showing his toned chest. He was a heartbreakingly sexy man, Sarah thought, but that wasn't why Sarah was attracted to him.

No, she was attracted to him because he was a good, kind man. And he was her person. She knew that from the start.

Before she ever knew a single thing about him, she knew

he was her person. It was just a sudden thing. Something Sarah always hoped would happen for her, but never did.

Until now.

"I feel ready to move on," he said. "I think Rita's been prodding me all along in your direction. Sometimes I swore I heard her whispering in my ear, urging me to contact you. But I always ignored it. I think she finally sent my best friend in my direction to get me out of my funk. Then she apparently sent me to this restaurant tonight because you were there." He shook his head. "It all sounds crazy, I know. But I now know that I wouldn't be betraying Rita if I moved on with you."

Sarah just stood there next to him, not saying a word. His hand was warm in hers, and she could almost hear his heart beating as he stood next to her.

"No," he said softly. "I wouldn't be betraying her if I moved on with you. I would be betraying her if I didn't. I somehow didn't figure that out until just now."

Sarah smiled and squeezed his hand.

Then she sighed as he leaned down and kissed her.

Oh, that kiss! She'd never felt such electricity coursing through her body until his soft lips met her own. She lost her breath briefly as the kiss became more urgent. He put his hands in her hair as he deepened the kiss, the water still raging around them.

After the kiss, Silas just stared at Sarah.

There were no words necessary. They were there together, under a full moon, their toes sinking deeply into the sand. Sarah would always remember this moment, she thought.

She would always remember the moment when she knew that the one she'd been waiting for was finally there.

And always would be.

Chapter Eighteen

Silas

Silas wasn't sure what words he would say to Sarah once they got on the beach. It wasn't like he rehearsed anything in his head. So he was surprised as anybody when he told Sarah that he thought Rita was talking to him all those months and that Rita sent Noah to him to try to prod him in her direction.

But, as he said those words, he realized he meant them. He hadn't even thought about it until that moment, but Rita really had been talking to him. It was through his dreams, as Rita appeared to him, happy and whole, telling him she was in a better place and she wanted him happy with Sarah. It was through the voice that was in his ears as he sat alone in his home, a drink in his hand, staring dispiritedly at the fire.

Then Noah appeared, seemingly out of nowhere. Yes, Noah decided to move to Los Angeles, but why? He had a good life in New York, and his wife, Suzy, had a thriving practice out there. Noah said he wanted to move to L.A. because he was tired of the pace and wanted to live by the beach again and just missed home. But was Rita pushing him out to the West Coast too? Rita knew Silas needed love and support, and he'd always gotten both things from Noah and Suzy.

And Noah was certainly working towards making Silas see that the best way to honor his late wife would be to lean into new love. Specifically, new love with Sarah.

And, as he stood there next to Sarah, holding her hand, feeling the fullness he used to feel with Rita, his heart coming back to life after feeling dead for so long - he knew that Rita was smiling at him. Finally, after all these months that she probably was disappointed and sad while watching him waste away, she was happy.

And so was he.

More by Ainsley Keaton

vinci-books.com/orchidislandbb

From betrayal to belonging: sisters find solace on the enchanting Orchid Island.

Three sisters—Paisley, Ivy and Skylar—seek comfort on Orchid Island. As they journey towards healing, each sister confronts her own struggles: Ivy's unfulfilled dreams, Paisley's longing for a family and Skylar's hidden traumas. Amidst the island's magic, the sisters also grapple with the disappearance of their father two decades ago. Will Orchid Island reveal long-buried secrets that could lead them to him?

Turn the page for a free preview…

The Orchid Island B&B: Chapter One

EILEEN

The girls need to be here. Eileen had been having vivid dreams lately, which always meant there was something in the universe she needed to pay attention to. And that something was that three of her granddaughters were in trouble and needed her.

Ivy was the first of her granddaughters she was worried about. At age 39, she was the oldest, and Eileen dreamed her entire life would fall apart. Eileen understood Ivy's pain because she had gone through one tragedy after another in her 75 years. However, Ivy would go through a painful awakening and Eileen knew she had to help her.

Paisley, at 38, one year younger than Ivy, was also going through a difficult period, but Eileen was less worried about her. What Paisley would endure was more of a necessary wake-up call, like a clanging alarm clock next to her bed. Even though she hadn't spoken to her in many years, Eileen knew Paisley was unhappy. Paisley had turned her back on her family and herself, lost her way and would have to find it again.

Skylar, 25, was the third granddaughter to undergo a life change. As with Paisley, Skylar had made a wrong turn. But Skylar's path was straightforward and she was young enough to bounce back.

Eileen sighed, realizing the universe would never give her more than she could handle. But she wondered why all three girls had to have a crisis in their lives simultaneously. Maybe that was all part of the plan.

Eileen knew that all three girls had made terrible choices in their lives. She wished she'd been able to convince them of such years ago, but she knew that even if she'd tried, her words of advice would've fallen on deaf ears. In the end, she realized that was the way it was with all people. Everybody, without exception, made mistakes that needed correcting. Falling in love with the wrong person, taking the wrong job, ignoring the wee inner voice - those were all part of the human condition.

Sometimes, the universe would attempt to throw a pebble at their proverbial windshield to warn them it was time to make a U-turn. If the pebble didn't do the trick, the universe would throw a boulder that broke the glass and sent the car into a tailspin.

Her granddaughters' proverbial cars were all going into a tailspin, and there was nothing that could be done about it. Yet, the girls, with their inherent strength, simply had to dust themselves off and realize they had the chance to make things right.

Eileen only hoped the three girls would take that chance, see it as an opportunity for personal growth, and make the most of it.

The Orchid Island B&B: Chapter Two

IVY

Ivy McAllister was burned out completely. She had been working 70 hours a week for a large law firm, McEnroe, Scully and Burrow, one of the largest firms in New York City. She was on the partnership track, but it seemed further away every year. She was 39 years old and had worked at this firm for the past 13 years and she had had enough.

She didn't even enjoy what she was doing. Her area of specialty was medical malpractice defense. That meant that when a patient was harmed by a doctor, she buried the other attorney with discovery requests to make that attorney give up. Of course, if anybody ever asked her firm's partners if that's what they were doing, burying the other attorney in discovery requests just because they wanted them to give up, they would deny it. But Ivy knew that's what they were doing.

Because Ivy hated what she was doing, her heart wasn't into it. That was why she was called into a meeting with the senior partners that day.

She knew what they would tell her without even really knowing it. She was about to be fired.

She sat down in the conference room and folded her hands.

"Ivy," Charles Delaney said to her when she sat down. "We need to speak with you about your performance."

"I know," Ivy said. "I understand."

"You haven't been putting in your billable hours," he said. We warned you about this six months ago, and you haven't raised them enough to satisfy us."

Ivy looked up. She had been staring at her hands since she got into the meeting. "Yes," she said. "I know I haven't been working the required 2,000 billable hour requirement. I've been working non-stop, but it just doesn't seem enough."

Charles nodded. "And you lost the last case you tried. Our client had to pay $100 million in that case."

Ivy nodded. "Yes," she said. "I know I lost that case, but our client was clearly negligent, bordering on criminally negligent. I think you know this." The case she lost involved a doctor who gave the wrong anesthesia to a patient who died on the table. The patient was clearly allergic to Propofol; it was clearly marked in the patient's medical records, and the doctor did not read the records before administering the anesthesia. Unfortunately, the patient who passed away was a prominent CEO with excellent earnings potential, which meant the damages would be astronomical. All this was known by the client beforehand, but he refused to settle. So Ivy had to try a dead-dog loser of a case, and, as she knew she would, she lost spectacularly.

"Of course," Charles said. "We all lose cases and know that case was a loser. But Ivy, that was just the latest..."

"Screw-up," she finished the sentence for him. "Go ahead and say it. I know I haven't had my head in the game, and I apologize."

She might have said "apologize," but she wasn't thinking it. She thought she was disgusted by what she did for this firm. She was responsible for countless individuals not getting the justice they deserved when they sued negligent doctors and pharmaceutical companies. She was having a hard time looking at herself in the mirror lately and she knew it.

Charles nodded. "You've been with this firm for thirteen years," he said, stating the obvious. "And, ordinarily, we would have offered you a partnership opportunity several years ago, as it is in our bylaws to offer our associates a partnership opportunity at their 10-year mark. We still cannot offer you a partnership opportunity, Ivy."

Ivy nodded. "And you want me out of the firm," she said.

"Yes," Charles said. "You haven't met our benchmarks for our associates and partners, both for the billable hours and the case win/loss percentages."

Ivy swallowed hard. Her $ 250,000-a-year income suddenly disappeared. "Okay," she said.

She felt like she was having an out-of-body experience for the rest of the afternoon. She met with the HR president, Rachel, who reviewed her severance package, which entitled her to just two months' salary.

Not that she was precisely in shock about the whole thing. No. She actually saw it coming for quite a long time. Her recent performance appraisals were the warning signs, and things went downhill since those performance appraisals. Still, it was humiliating. She'd worked for this firm since she left the University of Chicago Law School, the number three law school in the nation, just behind Stanford and Yale.

When she started law school, she was buzzed by everything about the experience. She read *One L*, which is virtually required reading for anybody entering an elite law school. It is the story of writer Scott Turow's first year at Harvard Law School. It is a harrowing read about the competition, the hours required to excel and the intolerable stress many first-year law students experience. It accurately describes the hazing-like atmosphere where burnout and dropping out often seem like attractive prospects.

But Ivy got through it and even thrived. Her outlines were stellar, the stuff other law students paid for, and they allowed her to graduate *Summa Cum Laude.* She made *Law Review* and was published on her first try. After graduating from law school, she dreamed of doing great things with her law degree. Maybe work for Legal Aid, helping the indigent sue slumlords or helping disabled people get benefits from the government. Perhaps working for the Sierra Club, suing polluters or working in environmental law for the government, ensuring environmental regulations are enforced.

Her plans were derailed by the reality of $100,000 + in student loans and an unexpected pregnancy. Her daughter Moira's father was often an out-of-work musician who contributed little financially to the household. Ivy had to go for the big bucks right out of law school. She had a daughter to raise and a husband to support, a husband who insisted on living in New York City because he was trying to make his career happen and wanted to be close to the action. She could not support everyone on a Sierra Club or government salary.

She really should've seen this moment coming right from the start. During the first five years, she never saw a courtroom. Her life was doing depositions, legal research, brief writing, and document analysis and production. It was soul-crushing work, 80 hours a week of toil and stress. If she worked in an area she believed in, she would've been energized by the work. But she felt she was working for the wrong side and couldn't shake that feeling. She was working for a firm of hired guns, and she knew a ton of little guys and ladies wouldn't see justice because of her firm's work. And she was a part of that.

So, in a way, the ax that fell on her neck was a relief.

At the same time, it was a stress. An enormous, awful stress. Now what? This job was the only one on her resume and she was kicked to the curb. That wouldn't look good. Not at all. She could just imagine interviewing for another job and trying to explain that she worked for this large firm for 13 years, never made partner, and was unceremoniously dumped because of performance issues. She would have to explain that she hated this kind of law so burnout was inevitable. Her resumé would be thrown into the circular file if she told any future partners this. As well it should be.

She absently doodled on a scrap of paper while Rachel performed the thankless job of explaining to Ivy about her severance package and COBRA health insurance, which was going to cost her $1,500 a month for herself, her husband and her daughter. Her job was paying for her insurance, of course, and now they wouldn't be, so that was one more thing Ivy would have to worry about once she was out on the street.

"Now, you had five weeks of sick leave you didn't use," Rachel explained. "So this is also included in your package."

Ivy nodded, feeling sick to her stomach. She was half listening, half looking out the window at the city below. Her office was on the 101st floor of One World Trade Center, one of the tallest buildings in the world. The view of the city from this high-up couldn't be beaten. That was one of the perks of her job because she could just go to the window of her office during her rare breaks and just stare at the city and imagine herself flying out the window. She would have wings, of course, in her imagination. She didn't actually imagine herself jumping to her death.

Rachel had to have known that Ivy wasn't listening to her, but she wasn't getting paid to have people actually listen. As long as Rachel was talking, she was doing her job. But Rachel was like that proverbial tree falling in the forest without a person to hear it. That was one of those conundrums that fascinated Ivy - if a tree falls in the forest without a person around, does it make a sound? Rachel was, indeed, making sounds but Ivy wasn't hearing them.

What was she doing with her life? What brought her here? Was she so insecure about her playwriting abilities that she gave up before she began? Because that was her dream, ever since she was a little girl - to be a playwright. Indeed, she had been writing plays since she was five years old. They were rudimentary, of course – how intricate of a play can a five-year-old write, after all - but it was really a form of escapism for her growing up.

But she certainly didn't believe she could make a living writing plays, so she went into law. And now, here she was—getting canned, being unceremoniously shown the door. Where did her sacrifice get her in the end? Because that's what this job was—a sacrifice for her family. She traded her personal happiness for her daughter and, to a lesser extent, her husband.

Rachel droned on and on about 401(k)s, the calculation of her severance pay, and other sundry items Ivy wasn't listening to. And after she talked to Rachel, she was subjected to the ignominy of the infamous exit interview. Since she was being fired, she was not prepared with questions for the partners. So she had to listen to the partners tell her precisely what was wrong with her performance and the things she did right. This was yet another humiliation in her mind. She was faced with all her failures as an attorney.

By the end of the day, Ivy felt about two feet tall. She remembered long ago when she used to be obsessed with the *Guinness Book of World Records* and read through the book about all the oddities in the world. There was a picture of a woman who was less than two feet tall, standing on a table. She felt like that woman right at that moment—tiny, insignificant.

And scared as hell.

After all was said and done, she took an Uber home and dismissed her sitter, Izzy, for the evening so she could take over.

"Thanks, Izzy," Ivy said. "I'm sorry I didn't get home sooner."

"You're fine," Izzy said. "I made dinner for Moira from the Blue Apron kit you bought. Grilled garlic shrimp with Spanish-style potatoes. I think that's one of her favorites."

Ivy's stomach was growling. She hadn't eaten all day. She hadn't had the time. She usually found a way to eat lunch at her desk, but she'd forgotten to pack anything, and she didn't have a second to go down to the food court in her building. So, she just didn't eat.

But garlic shrimp with Spanish-style potatoes sounded like they would hit the spot, so she rubbed her hands together excitedly.

"That sounds amazing," Ivy said. "I hope there are leftovers."

"Uh," Izzy began. "Actually, Brittany showed up for dinner, too, and—"

Ivy clenched her fists but took several deep breaths. She tried hard to put a smile on her face, but she knew it probably was more of a grimace.

"That's okay. I'll whip up some scrambled eggs or something," she said, her jaw clenched. It angered her that Brittany, of all people, ate the rest of that delicious meal. She disliked Brittany because she was a bad influence on her 13-year-old daughter. She remembered when Moira came home from Brittany's one day, completely sloshed.

Moira's excuse for drinking at Brittany's was that Brittany's billionaire dad had purchased a $3,000 bottle of Pappy Van Winkle bourbon, and she had to see what really expensive whiskey tasted like. This begged the question of whether the girl had a basis for comparison, which would mean she'd drunk whiskey before.

Izzy left, and Moira pirouetted into the living room. She was constantly practicing her ballet, even though the condo where they lived was so small that there wasn't enough room for her to do so. After all, this was the Upper West Side of Manhattan, and even her tiny condo was worth north of a million dollars.

Moira's muscular legs twirled her lean body around and around, her thick red curly hair—she got it from Ivy—tied tightly on top of her head.

"Hi, Mom," she said as she spun around and around.

"Hi yourself," Ivy said. "You're getting outstanding, by the way."

"I hope so. I'm up for the lead in our recital in three months."

"I'm sure you'll get it." Ivy opened up the fridge and saw the eggs were gone. Damn! She was suddenly starving for scrambled eggs with cheddar cheese.

"The eggs are gone," Moira said, stating the obvious. "Brittany needed them for a cake she's baking for her mom's birthday."

"You mean her mother actually consumes something other than alcohol?" Ivy asked.

"Sometimes. I mean, not really, but she likes chocolate cake."

Ivy put her head against the fridge. "There's nothing in there to eat."

"You haven't been to the store," Moira said.

"You're right. I haven't had time to breathe," Ivy said. She suddenly felt tears coming to her eyes. "I obviously need a personal assistant who can do grocery shopping for me. And apparently, a housekeeper because I don't have time to clean up this sty of a house, and you and your father obviously don't care enough to pick up after yourselves."

The place *was* a sty. Moira's dirty clothes were strewn all over the floor in front of the washer and dryer, usually walled off from the living room by French doors. The French doors were open, showing the clothes. Kevin's magazines were all over both the coffee and dining room tables.

Also on the dining room table were several pairs of shoes—Moira's and Kevin's. At least a week's worth of mail covered the kitchen counter. A bathroom towel was randomly thrown over the shade of the floor lamp. Moira had apparently thrown several jackets on the sofa. As for

Kevin, he seemed to have found a home for his jackets on one of the dining room chairs.

Ivy glanced at the sink, which was filled with dirty dishes. None were hers, as she hadn't been eating at home much.

"The dishwasher is busted?" Ivy asked.

"No, why?" Moira asked. Her long leg was on the kitchen counter, and she was grabbing her foot with her left hand while her right hand stretched above her head.

"Then what's up with the dishes in the sink?"

Moira stood up long enough to shrug. "The dishwasher is full."

Ivy closed her eyes. "Then put the dishes in the dishwasher away," she said through gritted teeth. "Seriously, Moira, I need some help."

"Mom, you're like never around. As in never. Maybe if you were around, you'd get this place the way you want."

Ivy glared at her daughter, not wanting to say the words on her tongue. Her therapist, whom she usually saw online because she never had time to go into her office, always instructed her not to be combative with her daughter. She was supposed to channel her anger inward.

"You're right. I'm never around. Of course, I have to work all the time because I'm paying for the taxes on this home, the food you eat, your private school, your ballet lessons and socking away money for your college. You want to go to Juilliard, right? You know that school is currently $75,000 a year if you count room and board, and by the time you get there, it'll probably be $100,000 yearly. Or more. I work constantly because I don't want you saddled with a half-million in debt before you even reach a professional stage. So, the least you can do, and I mean the very least you can do, is pick up after yourself, don't give away all my food, and put the damn dishes in the dishwasher away."

At that, Moira glared at Ivy and slammed open the dishwasher door. Then she made a show of banging each drinking glass into the cupboard and clanging each dish on top of the other into a different cupboard. Then she banged the cupboard doors shut so hard that Ivy was surprised they remained on their hinges. The silverware drawer was pulled savagely open, and then Moira threw the knives, forks, and spoons into the silverware separator.

"There," Moira said. "You happy?"

"Obviously—"

"I'm going to my room," she said. "I'll be practicing ballet, so don't bother me."

Ivy sighed. Moira was getting more and more moody these days. Then again, she was 13. That age was the very worst. Not quite an adult, not quite a child, with hormones going crazy. Her daughter was growing up. And Moira just got her period, Ivy thought sadly. That probably was the reason for the childish tantrum she just threw.

Where did the time go? It seemed like just yesterday that Ivy was dropping Moira off at her kindergarten, with Moira begging not to go. She was afraid of going to kindergarten, fearful of the unknown. As many children are. Ivy was also terrified of going to kindergarten, and her mother assured her it would be fine. Of course, it was - Ivy's kindergarten teacher taught her how to share, nap, and play games. Ivy imagined that was how her entire school life would be - recess, playing games, listening to music, taking naps and hearing stories.

Of course, the reality hit the following year when Ivy entered 1st grade and had to learn stuff. But kindergarten was fun, and Ivy was no longer scared after that first day.

Moira had the same fears Ivy had when Ivy dropped her off that first day - it was just unknown. Moira had never really been out of the apartment for any length of time as she always had a nanny come in and watch her while Ivy worked. But, just like Ivy, Moira came back from that first day all aglow and excitedly told Moira about how much fun kindergarten was.

Now, here Moira was, a beautiful, tall, red-headed teenager with an occasional attitude. And Moira would soon be dating, driving and doing everything Ivy didn't want to even think about. After all that, her daughter would be out of the nest, which filled Ivy with dread.

But Moira was here now, and Ivy finally had time to spend with her daughter. Yes, they would be broke if Ivy couldn't find a comparable job, but there was the possibility that Ivy could find a job where she could spend more time with her daughter.

A woman could dream, couldn't she?

But she would have to downsize if she wanted to not work a million hours a week. She would have to sell the condo and move someplace else. She owned her condo - she was fortunate to be able to pay it off in just 10 years and was really lucky the value had gone up so much in those 10 years - but living in the city was just too expensive. And she had nothing in savings or retirement, as every penny she earned over the years went to paying off the condo, living expenses, supporting her husband's dreams, Moira's private school and nanny and putting enough money into Moira's 529 college savings plan. She had to fully fund Moira's plans for going to Juilliard, which was currently $75,000 a year and would undoubtedly be much more by the time Moira arrived.

Then she wondered about Kevin. What was he doing?

She couldn't remember if he had a gig that night or if he was just in rehearsals. At any rate, although he worked long hours, he didn't get paid nearly enough to allow Ivy to ease up on her own hours.

Then, she saw it. A letter with her name on it. It was on one of the few surfaces not cluttered with junk - a lamp stand next to the couch.

With shaking hands, she opened up the envelope and read.

Ivy,

I haven't found the words to express my feelings. You haven't been home enough for me to talk to you, even if I wanted to. But we both know it's not right between us and hasn't been right for a long time.

I'm in love with somebody else and want to marry her immediately. I'm so sorry for this. I know we tried, but we're just too different. We never should've gotten together, although we did make a beautiful daughter, so I can't regret my time with you.

Now, I know you'll obsess about what you did wrong, so I'm just going to say you did nothing wrong. You just have personality traits that don't vibe with mine. You're too anal, too driven, too much of a workaholic. You literally cannot relax. I can't remember the last time I've been able to watch a movie with you without you constantly sending emails on your phone while the movie is on. I don't know when I've been able to sit down at dinner with you without you typing on your laptop while we're trying to eat. We've talked about taking a vacation for years, but you can never get away.

Also, I'm going to Europe to see if I can make a living there. I think I can find success in the UK; there's more of a market for my music there.

I want to live my life freer than you. I should've known when we met that a Virgo and a Sagittarius could never get along. It wasn't even oil and water. It was literally fire and earth.

Please, find another Virgo, or maybe a Capricorn or a Taurus. You'll be much happier; trust me on this.

With all my love (and I do still love you),

Kevin

Ivy stared at the note and realized Kevin's shoes were still on the dining room table. She should've been upset by this note, but she wasn't. She and Kevin hadn't been good for a long time, nor had they seen one another much lately. The note seemed to be just something stating the obvious to her and, like with her getting canned today from the law firm, it felt like a relief.

Ivy shook her head. Well, Kevin was gone. It was a bit of a shock but not necessarily unpleasant, and Ivy felt sad about that. He'd been her husband for the past 13 years—they married shortly after Moira was born. And they married *only* because Moira was born, so that was the problem. Kevin was right—they really were oil and water all along—or earth sign and fire sign, as Kevin noted.

Ivy sighed. She felt defeated. And she suddenly faced the reality of a divorce - she would have to give Kevin half of everything she owned. Although New York was an equitable distribution state, which meant that property would need to be divided up equitably, as opposed to 50/50, as some states divide up property, she knew that Kevin, having very little income, would be entitled to quite a bit of what they owned. Generally, it was against public policy to leave one spouse destitute in the event of a divorce, even if that spouse was the man. So she knew she would have to give up quite a bit to her deadbeat husband.

And, all at once, it just became too much. It all hit her - she was out of a job, out of a husband, would soon have to pay a divorce attorney and would have to take out a considerable home equity loan to get the money to pay off Kevin. She still had a kiddo at home to take care of and expensive ballet lessons for her young daughter. Not to mention tuition for Moira's private school - Moira was enrolled at the prestigious Adelphi Academy in Brooklyn, a school chosen for its strong dance program.

Then, she did something that was out of the ordinary for her.

She started screaming.

The Orchid Island B&B: Chapter Three

IVY

"Mom!" Moira said when she came running into Ivy's bedroom. "What's wrong? What's going on?"

"I'll have to sell you to a weird family like Cosette in *Les Miserables.* Or sell you for scientific experiments."

Then Ivy started to laugh. One of her favorite movies was Monty Python's *The Meaning of Life.* One of her favorite skits in that movie was where the man had hundreds of children. He ended up selling them for scientific experiments after he lost his job. Whenever she thought about the scene where the stork drops the new baby to the floor, and the mother says, "Can you pick that up for me?" as she was washing dishes, Ivy giggled.

"Mom, Cosette wasn't sold to anybody. She was given to that weird family by her hooker mother. But good job with that second reference." Moira loved that Monty Python movie, too. Like Ivy's, her humor was off-beat and just a tad dark. "But why are you saying this?"

"Because, well, we're broke. We're broke, my job is gone, and I have no desire to work for another large firm."

She felt like she was cracking up, yet she had to keep it together. That was what she did. She kept it together, no matter what life threw at her. She would've been in the loony bin long ago if she hadn't.

"Yeah, Mom, I told you you were doing the devil's work helping all those rich dudes get out of their shady dealings."

"And other large firms are just the same. They operate for one reason and one reason only - to help wealthy people get away with crimes." And that was true - big law firms represented doctors who killed their patients, pharmaceutical companies who manufactured harmful drugs, tobacco companies who destroyed lungs, and polluters who obliterated the environment.

Some represented companies who wanted to merge, but plenty of little people got hurt and lost their jobs even in those cases.

"Yeah, Mom, you don't go and work for those firms who represent The Man," Moira said, nodding. "By the way, I'm sorry for my brattiness earlier. I'm 13. I'm supposed to be moody, right?"

"Right," Ivy said. Her stomach started to knot and she wondered if she was going to get sick. "It's not a problem. Your brattiness, I mean." She felt herself gag. "Excuse me."

She ran into the bathroom and perched over the toilet. Nothing came out, however. *Of course. I haven't eaten today.*

"Mom," Moira said outside the bathroom door. "Are you okay?"

Ivy stood up and opened the door. "No. I'm not." She started to wring her hands. "What am I going to do?" She shook her head. "I'm going to have to just suck it up and get a job with another large firm, that's what. I have to keep up this place, and your school, ballet lessons, and nanny. I was barely making ends meet on my salary, so I must find another job with another large firm."

But the very thought filled her with dread. She was so unhappy at that firm. Her life wasn't her own. It belonged to the almighty billable hour.

Besides, after word got around that she was unceremoniously fired, she would be radioactive to all other large firms. She could work at a small firm, for Legal Aid or do some kind of criminal defense work, but those jobs would not pay the bills. Moira's private school alone was $40,000 a year, about what she would make at Legal Aid.

"Mom, tell me what's going on," Moira said.

Ivy took a deep breath. "Your father is gone."

"What do you mean he's gone?" Moira's voice was suddenly tiny, barely above a whisper. "Mom, what do you mean he's gone?"

"He's gone. He's in Europe. Something about trying to make it there with his band because there's more of a market for his music." This might be true, as Kevin's band was a punk-pop band in the mold of My Chemical Romance or Green Day, a style of music that passed the United States sometime in the past 20 years. She had no idea if the English still had a taste for that kind of music, but they probably did.

Moira blinked away tears. "Gone. Dad's gone." She ran back into her room and slammed the door again.

Ivy took a deep breath. She almost knew how her daughter felt. After all, her father disappeared, too. Except he vanished without a trace and without a word to anyone. Nobody in the family knew what had happened to him. All she or her sisters knew was that one day he just disappeared as if he'd never existed.

She suspected her mother knew what had happened to

him, but she was a vault if she did. She maintained that she was as mystified as Ivy and her sisters were about what had happened to Rory Connelly.

The hole in Ivy's heart that was left by her father leaving like that was immeasurable and had never healed. Her father was a good man - kind, patient and loving. Basically the opposite of her mother, who was none of those things. He was always merry, too, with a great sense of humor and fun, playing practical jokes and spinning wild tales of his youth in Ireland.

She went and knocked on Moira's door. "Moira," she said. "Can I come in?"

Moira didn't answer, so Ivy opened the door.

Her daughter was lying on the bed, face down, her head towards the wall. "Go away," she said through tears.

Ivy sat down on the bed. "Moira, honey, I know how you feel."

"No, you don't."

"I do. My father left when I was young, too, remember?"

"You weren't young. You were in college."

"I was, that's true. But I still needed him. I never stopped needing him. And I loved my father very much."

Moira sat up. "Why did he leave me?"

"He didn't leave you, Pooh Bear. He left me. He left a note."

"A note? A note?" Moira's face was confused, with her green eyes scrunched up and she was biting her lower lip. "How could he just leave you a note? I mean, I've had boys break up with me by text, which is the lamest thing in the whole world. But you guys were married. For years. How could he?"

Ivy tapped her fingers on Moira's bedpost. She couldn't

meet her daughter's eyes. "I guess it could've been worse. He could've just taken off like my father did and not given an explanation. At least I kind of know where he is - the UK. So, if I wanted to find him, to, you know, kill him, I might have some degree of success in that."

"What did that note say?" Moira asked.

"Let me get it for you."

Ivy went into the living room and, with shaking hands, picked up the note. She brought it into Moira's room and handed it to her.

"Here," Ivy said. "Read it and try not to weep."

Moira read the note and then handed it back to Ivy. "Lame." She shook her head. "That's some trifling and shady stuff right there, Mom."

"It is that." Ivy took a deep breath. "So, extra money will be nonexistent unless I find something else tout de suite."

Moira scrunched up her eyebrows, and Ivy could read her mind.

"Don't worry, Juilliard is still paid for," Ivy said. "Don't worry about that. I opened up an educational trust when you were born. But, as for the two of us—"

"Scientific experiments for the lot of you!" Moira said in a British accent.

Ivy smiled. "Are you going to be okay?" she asked.

Moira shrugged one of her shoulders. "How okay am I supposed to be? My dad just took off. What are we going to do?"

"We'll figure it out," Ivy said.

Ivy went into the living room. As she did, she passed by a picture of her and her sister, Paisley. They were standing next to the oak tree on her Gran Eileen's estate on Orchid Island.

As she looked at that picture, memories flooded back to her. It was taken well before her life had spun out of control.

Ivy closed her eyes and saw her grandmother's beautiful house by Emerald Beach, a private beach on Orchid Island, just off the coast of Rhode Island. The beautiful isle was named for the colorful wild orchids that grew in bogs all around the island.

Gran Eileen's home was a rambling Cape Cod mansion less than a block from the beach, yet the place seemed miles away from anywhere. There were acres of land on which she and her sister Paisley played, and later, the twins, Skylar and Liliana, were born. But by the time they were born, Paisley and Ivy were ten and eleven years old, respectively, so Ivy didn't have early childhood memories that involved playing with them.

But she and Paisley played on the grounds yearly because that was where they stayed during the summers. Gran didn't work, and their engineer mother didn't have time for them when they were out of school.

Ivy had looked forward to those summers on the island like she looked forward to nothing else in her life. There were endless ways to entertain herself, such as the colossal willow tree Ivy climbed to the top. She would get scared once she was on the top of the tree and sometimes thought the fire department would need to be called to get her down. But, the next day, she would be back at it, climbing it once again.

About the Author

Ainsley Keaton lives with her hubby and two fur-babies in Southern California. When she's not binge-watching *Grace and Frankie*, *Succession* and *Downton Abbey*, she's reading historical and women's fiction and scouring the beach for sea glass and sand dollars.

Thanks for reading!

www.ingramcontent.com/pod-product-compliance
Lightning Source LLC
La Vergne TN
LVHW030625241026
850939LV00032B/493
* 9 7 8 1 0 3 6 7 0 3 8 0 6 *